WHISTLE IN THE DARK

SUSAN HILL LONG

Holiday House / New York

Printed and Bound in April 2014 at Maple Press, York, PA, USA.
www.holidayhouse.com
3 5 7 9 10 8 6 4 2

Library of Congress Cataloging-in-Publication Data.
Hill, Susan, 1965–
Whistle in the dark / by Susan Long. — First edition.
pages cm
Summary: In a small Missouri town during the 1920s, Clem is torn
between family responsibility and the life he wishes to lead when he must
begin working in the lead mine on his thirteenth birthday to help pay for
his sister's medical care.
ISBN 978-0-8234-2839-7 (hardcover)
[1. Coming of age—Fiction.   2. Lead mines and
mining—Fiction.]   I. Title.
PZ7.H55742Wh 2013
[Fic]—dc23
2012034507

ISBN 978-0-8234-3191-5 (paperback)

For my dad, Ronald W. Hill

CONTENTS

1. The Last Day   1
2. The First Day   10
3. Happy Birthday   26
4. Pally-Boy   40
5. The Woods   46
6. Lindy   53
7. Treasures   61
8. A Cave Pearl   66
9. A Thing of Beauty   75
10. The Bell Tree   78
11. The Cardinal   88
12. Losers, Weepers   94
13. An Accident   101
14. Crackers   111
15. A Dress   120
16. Finders, Keepers   122
17. Stories and Lies   131
18. March 18   137
19. After the Storm   148
20. The School Yard   152
21. *Glückauf*   158
22. The Evening News   167
23. To Grass   174

1

THE LAST DAY

IT WAS JUNE, the middle of the day Clem was to quit
being a boy.

They were all in rows watching Miss Bedelia Pipe chalk
out on the board a problem Clem wasn't going to bother
with. Normally he would, but not today. Clem stared out
the window at the sky, clear and blue until it bumped against
the rocky knob of Goggin Mountain.

The classroom windows opened onto the redbuds that
marked the edges of the dry playground, but there was no
breeze coming in. Clem sighed deeply, and picked up the
scent of the lone bull pine that towered over the school
yard's western boundary, a tree foreign to these parts, its
seed dropped by a tornado some years back. He smelled,
too, the dusty heat of packed dirt, and the lead of the pen-
cil, and also a whiff of something different, maybe some
rain on the way, and he filled his chest with all of it, as if
he might never smell those normal kinds of things again.

He heard the small sound of someone standing
beside him, and opened his eyes on Miss Pipe, framed by

the window. One hand held papers against her dress; the other hand she reached out to Clem as if to say *Come along,* or maybe *Stay put.* His heart took a little jump under his shirt buttons. She was a slim person who seemed big to Clem, with yellow hair and smooth, pink skin. A small line gathered between her eyes, and her mouth went up at the corners like a smile, but thin.

"Yes, Miss Pipe?"

Her mouth opened as if she was going to say something. But she only riffled the papers, nodded, handed back Clem's paper, and went on down the row.

The assignment had been to write two hundred fifty words on the topic "I believe…" Clem had tried to remember the things Miss Pipe lectured about. Use metaphor and simile, choose descriptive words and action words, avoid the run-on sentence. Across the top margin of his paper was written an *A* and one comment in Miss Pipe's firm lettering: *Good Luck.*

"Clemson Harding, because this is your last day, I've chosen you to read your paper aloud," Miss Pipe said now.

Bad luck, Clem thought. Awkwardly, he pushed himself sideways to clear the desktop with his knees, stood, and walked to the front of the room. He turned to face the class, clutching the paper in his hands. Only three students were really looking at him. Mickey Olsen waggled his eyebrows to try and make him laugh. His sister, Esther, smiled, waiting, her hands clasped in front of her. The third person looking at him, from behind a curtain of thick black hair, was Linda Jean, the girl everybody poked fun at because she wore dirty clothes and repeated the first grade and, worse, because of a scar that sealed the skin of half her face. Behind her back they called her Frankenstein, or just Frank. He wondered, not for the first time, what on earth had happened to tear open her cheek—there were tales of a chimney fire, a jagged hunting knife, an explosion. He gripped the sides of his paper in front of him and began to read out loud.

"I'm awake but I don't know it yet." Clem glanced up over the top of the paper at Miss Pipe, then down again. "I hear the tang, tang, tang of the woodhen knocking on the chimney cap, and the rattle of beak on tin snaps my eyelids up like roller shades, and I'm out of bed and out of the house and I'm feeling the damp on my skin and I'm feeling the sun red hot on my eyelids. The small gritty bits of earth under the soles of my bare feet don't trouble me at all. I run flying toward the creek in the woods. I run there so much I've worn out a path in the ground getting to the water. In the trees I run slow and light, because the ground is springy with fallen things and growing things. I'm dodging trees and panting like a dog, which is something I believe I want more than anything in the world. I get to the creek and I drop to my knees in the spongy place along the bank and I lower my head and reach my hands into the creek like a cup. I see myself, but the water is nothing like a mirror. I can't make my face out to be anything but a shadow. Now I splash creek water on my face and it's so cold and sharp it almost hurts. It takes my breath clean away."

Clem glanced up again. Esther was looking right at him. She grinned and nodded encouragement. He did not return her smile.

"I believe that a person should get up as early as possible, especially in summer," he went on. "I believe a person should be wide awake."

Two hundred fifty words exactly, including the wood-hen thumping, if anybody wanted to count. Clem put his head down and hurried back to his seat. People clapped because that is what they do when some poor kid has to get up and read in front of everybody like that.

And that was how it ended, Clem's last day of school. He felt in a way pleased, everybody clapping as if he'd done something special. But he knew he hadn't done anything except what he was told to do. And now he was still doing what he was told, following in Pap's footsteps.

He packed up his pencils and his papers and his dinner pail, and he and Esther walked right out the door as easy as if it didn't mean a thing. Clem half thought someone would stop him. He walked by Miss Pipe and she put her arm out straight. He took her hand and pumped it once, up-down, as he'd been taught, and then let go.

"Stop by and visit when you can," she said, squinting into the sun and shading her eyes with her hand. "You're a good student, Clem. I don't know if I've known a boy so in love with books and words."

Clem blushed a little from that stuff about being in love.

"I will," he said.

"Wait a moment, I've got something for you," Miss Pipe said. She disappeared into the schoolhouse, returned a moment later, and handed him a book.

"*Peter Pan*," she said.

Clem took the book and narrowed his eyes at the cover illustration. "Fairies?"

"One fairy," she said, laughing lightly the way Clem thought a fairy might, "and a horrible pirate called Captain

Hook, and a crocodile, and a very clever boy." She smiled at Clem. "You read it, and tell me what you think."

Clem looked down at her, he'd got that tall, and he nodded. "Thank you, Miss Pipe." He tucked the book into his dinner pail, then he walked away and stood at the edge of the school yard.

Clem folded his essay paper longwise and beat the hard crease of it against his thigh, watching Mickey and Junie and the other kids scatter the way they did every day after school. Tomorrow, Mickey and Junie and the rest—Esther, too, if she was up to it—and Miss Pipe in one of her clean, pale dresses, they'd all be back here again. Not Clem.

The insides of Clem's eyelids stung and he blinked them hard.

"What's all that stuff about being awake?"

It was Mickey. Mickey was small, with the pale white skin of someone mostly kept inside. He wore a new white shirt, pressed in the morning but damp and wrinkled now. The shirttails had pulled out in places from his neat short pants, and his mother would get after him later, Clem knew, tell him he looked like a roughneck.

Clem tapped his paper against his leg again and shrugged. Then he crushed the assignment into a ball and pitched it away into the bushes at the edge of the school yard.

"Well, you're a lucky stiff, that's what I know," Mickey said.

"You reckon?" Clem figured Mickey was the lucky one, for more reasons than he could count, but chief among them being that he had a dog, a big dumb yellow one, all for himself.

"Doing real work, earning real money." Mickey hitched his book strap over his shoulder and dug the toe of his Buster Brown into the dirt.

Clem's eyelids began to smart again. He rubbed one eye with the heel of his hand. "It's hard work, I guess," he said. He pushed at Mickey's books. "You'll get strong, too," he said, and punched him in the arm.

"Right." Mickey smiled with half his mouth and rubbed his shoulder. "There goes old Frankenstein," he said, jutting his chin to where Linda Jean made her measured, unhurried way across the playing field. A small band of classmates trailed her, lurching stiff-legged with arms outstretched, their faces twisted into ugly masks. If Linda Jean was aware of her tormenters, she didn't let on: she didn't glance over her shoulder, she didn't hurry.

"What's that she's whistling?" Mickey wondered aloud.

Clem hummed along, trying to place the tune. Then he smiled. "It's 'Hail, Hail, the Gang's All Here,'" he said, turning to Mickey.

Mickey grinned, and together they sang the chorus. "What the heck do we care, what the heck do we care!"

When Clem glanced again across the playing field, Linda Jean was disappearing into the woods on the other side, the ragged hem of her dress a flash of red among the gray maples, and the Frankensteins were drifting around the edge of the school yard like water skeeters going to bump into some other trouble.

"Well, see ya, Clem. Stay awake, whatever that means."

"See ya, Mickey."

Mickey straggled away across the playground, kicking up clouds of dust; Mickey's mother would wipe his shoes clean later and buff them to a shine. Clem couldn't remember when he'd last got a pair of new boots. He called across the school yard to his sister. When Esther turned, her flowered dress swung around her knees, and her hair, as fair as Clem's was dark, floated for a moment, then settled on her shoulders. At nine, Ettie was taller and wispier than other girls her age, and she had pale skin and small, fine features, except for her clear blue eyes, large and set wide as if she was always catching sight of something new. She walked to Clem when he called her a second time, and put out her hand to hold his.

Clem turned his shoulder and didn't take her hand. If not for Esther, he wouldn't be in this spot, he thought. It was the same thought he'd had many times since he'd been told he had to go down the mines. If not for her he could stay put in school and play outfield instead of Mickey, who would only drop the ball every time, they'd see.

A train sounded from east of town. The train went through twice a day, but nobody ever got off in Leadanna, Missouri, and nobody ever boarded. Only the ore moved on. People on their way to St. Louis, or Chicago, or even New York City, they probably didn't even look out the window. The whistle sounded again, starting low and rising, then gone.

"Come on," Clem said, and Ettie fell in beside him. He took big steps so she'd have a hard time keeping up. The two of them walked away down Main, then turned left on First Street toward home. At one end of town was the Charles A. Snow school, and at the other end was the St. James Lead Company's American B mine and the mill, and in between, First Street, Second Street, Third, Miller, all struggled to stay in neat lines as they rolled up and over the ridges of limestone buried in great shelves below. The residential streets were lined with mostly one-story houses, each with one or two front steps and a saggy porch and bare or peeling or painted clapboard siding, all the same, and some of them, down along Miller Street, Company owned. On Main Street, closer to the mine, huddled a little gathering of businesses: Miller's Store and the Tunnel Tavern, and Travers' All-Day Breakfast. From here, Clem could see the giant chat dump looming over the other edge of town. Beyond that squatted the lead mine, where at this time of day Pap was still on his shift, and where their grandfather, Pap's daddy, had worked till the miners' consumption made him sick enough he couldn't go down anymore.

Clem stopped and stared at the great mound of the chat dump. It looked solid, permanent, as honest a mountain as old Taum Sauk. But it was really just grains of sand, piled there by miners like Pap and Grampy turning the earth inside out. One good puff of God could blow it all away.

"You okay?" Esther asked. Clem looked at her. She looked like Mickey's big yellow dog, her head cocked to one side, hoping for a sign he wasn't mad. He shifted his dinner pail to the other hand. He wasn't mad, not really. It wasn't her fault.

"Sure," he said. "I'm fine."

"Liar."

She laughed and grabbed his hand in her small ones. At first he roughly curled his fingers under so she couldn't see. He knew she wanted to count the white spots on his fingernails and see how many lies he told. But Ettie's fingers pried at his; sorry for acting mean to her, he fanned his fingers out.

She counted under her breath. "Six!" she said. She dropped his hand and counted on her own fingers. "A gift, a ghost, a friend, a foe, a letter to come." That was five fingers, one hand. Then the thumb on the other hand, stuck up skyward as if to say *Okay!* She looked up at her big brother. "A journey to go. That's for six," she said. "Your fortune."

Clem nodded. "Okay, Ettie," he said. "Let's go."

Tomorrow would be Clem's birthday. He knew to the minute what time he was born because his mother remembered those moments, particulars that might be taken for signs. She had often told him how she used to watch to see if her children smiled in their sleep, an omen that meant they were talking to the angels and planning to leave her.

June 2, 1924. He would turn thirteen years old at exactly eleven in the morning, and he would be completely in the dark.

2

THE FIRST DAY

THE FIRST DAY on the job started out smelling like biscuits. Clem got up quietly and dressed quickly. He tucked his checkered work shirt into his waist overalls, then did up the shoulder straps and ran a hand over his chest to try and calm his heart. He looked around, at his cot with its blue blanket and white sheet, and beside the cot, the wooden crate that was his bedside table and bookshelf. Clem's stomach turned over and he wished he could get back into bed, pull up the sheet, and read books all day long.

He glanced over at the brown wool blanket that divided the room. Behind it Ettie still slept. Later she'd go to school. She would read and eat dinner at her desk or in the shade of the big silver maple, and she'd play outside on the field, and all the while he'd be down the mine, under the ground, in the dark. Clem looked at the book gripped in his two hands; then he let the book drop. *Crack*. He glared at the heavy blanket and then he turned and left the room.

In the kitchen Pap stood waiting for him, along with

Ma and Grampy. In Pap's hands was a brand new miner's cap and lamp. He held it out and nodded.

"Happy birthday, Clem," Pap said.

The tan canvas cap seemed big and brutal, somehow, something he'd wear into battle—like his boots, Red Wing Number Sixteens, standard issue in the War. When he put on the cap, he was surprised that it fit okay. He wished he could see himself in a mirror. He took the cap off and glanced at his face in the lamp's round reflector. He could see only one eyeball and part of his nose. He ran his fingers across the nickel-plated Justrite logo, and examined how the hook and braces held the lamp onto the cap's leather patch above the bill.

"The carbide lamp with the daylight beam," Pap said, quoting a familiar advertisement. He was unusually chipper.

"The lamp that puts daylight underground!" Grampy yelled. He was part deaf and yelled everything. "I'd thought to give you mine, but your old man had rather spend a dollar and get you a brand new one all your own." Grampy began to cough. He tugged a square white handkerchief from his back pocket and lowered himself into a kitchen chair.

Pap looked proudly at the lamp in Clem's hands. "It's got a windproof cover on the tip, there, Clemson," he said, speaking over Grampy's coughing. "I filled up the carbide chamber already." Clem looked past Grampy at the shelf above the front door where Pap always kept his Shapleigh .30-30 and a box of shells, and a couple of two-pound tins of carbide—the familiar red, white, and blue of the Union Carbide label, or the green Shawinigan, with their warnings in big block letters: KEEP DRY. FLAMMABLE. EXPLOSIVE. HARMFUL. The words made alarms go off inside Clem's head. How could they send him down there? Harmful! Explosive!

Ma leaned and kissed him on the cheek and he turned to her. She dabbed at her eyes and smiled weakly at him.

"Have a good first day," she said. "We'll mark your birthday tonight." She wrapped two biscuits in a white cloth and handed him the small bundle, plus a sack of clean clothes and the dinner pail she'd packed. Pap and Clem left the house. Clem turned once and saw Ma still standing in the doorway. She waved a dish towel above her head. Clem raised his dinner pail, then turned his back on home.

The air at that hour, six thirty, was cool and damp, clammy on Clem's cheeks. Clouds covered the early sun, and a chilling breeze swept fingers of mist around their legs as Clem and Pap came up over the rise and then walked down into town past Miller's. Pap strode right along. He wasn't that tall, but his legs were long, and Clem had to run a few steps every little while to keep up. Pap held his head high. His thick hair, cut close, looked like a black knit cap.

"Best part of the day, right here, Clemson," he said. He turned and nodded at Clem. "I've been looking forward to this day," he continued. "It's what we do, the Harding men, we're miners, and I'm pleased to have you alongside me now."

Mouth full of biscuit, Clem didn't answer. He could hear that Pap was talking, his low voice ranging up and down, up and down, but he barely heard the words. Every other day of the week up until today he'd been heading in the exact other direction. He turned and walked backward, facing up the hill toward the school. Even from here he could see the tip-top of the great bull pine just west of school.

They walked by Travers' All-Day Breakfast, and Clem looked in the windows at the people eating eggs and sausages, drinking hot coffee. There was the door. He could just step through that door and sit down at a table, and maybe the day wouldn't happen. But his feet kept moving toward the American B mine. One more glance in the window showed him Lonnie Travers pouring coffee for a customer, smiling in a pretty way that reminded him of his teacher, Miss Pipe.

"Clemson?" Clem realized Pap's rambling voice had lifted and was hanging in the air.

"What?" He looked blankly at Pap.

"I said, are you pleased?" Pap's expression was sober, as always, but bright, expectant. Clem slowed his step, and Pap walked ahead. Pleased? How could he be? "Well come on, then," Pap said over his shoulder. Clem hurried to catch up, his dinner pail banging against the side of his thigh.

"Oh, I know it might not seem like much, heading down for a long day of it like we are," Pap said, his voice warming in a way Clem wasn't used to. "But I tell you what, Clemson—we're part of it. The two of us, now, we're part of the land, part of the Ozark Mountains themselves."

Clem swallowed hard, and tried for a joke. "I'd rather be part of Wappapello Lake, fishing for crappie."

Pap was silent.

Clem sighed, almost a groan. "Or part of my own

backyard, playing fetch with the dog I don't have." It came out whiny. He kicked a stone down the street ahead of them.

"You know your ma won't have a dog," Pap said. "She spoils you plenty, boy, but"—he frowned—"no dog."

Clem swung his dinner pail in an arc. "She wouldn't even have to do anything. I'd keep him outside, Pap! I'd feed him and take good care of him—"

Pap held up a hand and pursed his lips.

Clem caught up to the stone and kicked it again.

Now the chat dump rose up like the hump of a ridgy-backed beast ahead of them, making the buildings look insignificant.

"It taunts the olden peaks that pen it in and give it birth," Clem said. Pap scowled at him.

"It's from a poem. I wrote it for school."

Pap grunted. "Poetry is beside the point," he said. "Makes it sound silly." Then he frowned. "Miss Pipe says you're sharp, and I know it, Clem. I know it, with the high marks and the reading. Heck, you already read more books than I ever did."

Clem kicked the stone ahead.

"I've always been proud to be a miner. You'll take to it. The lead's the only game in town, Clem, and we need the money. If we didn't, I'd let you grow up 'n be a doctor." Clem's heart leaped. Maybe he could turn around right now and go back. Maybe Pap wouldn't make him go down into the deep dark.

"Be good to have a doctor in the house," Pap said, but his voice had gone hard. Then he laughed.

Pap was only joking, then, about being a doctor. Clem

shifted his dinner pail to the other hand and cut a glance at Pap. Clem could see he was thinking of Esther, and the bills.

Now Clem looked up at the chat conveyor that ran like a scar up the steep slope. Rail cars dumped their loads of rocky debris even at this hour. If his feet kept moving, he was really going to go down there and fill those very rail cars. He watched as one car dumped its load of spent rock and earth.

They followed the road around the great mountain of the chat pile, and when Clem saw the rolling mill, the powder shack, the office, the headframe rising stark as a gallows against the sky, any poetic thought left him. It was everything exactly the same as he'd seen a hundred times before, but it all looked different. Dirtier and older, and ominous, like ruins.

About fifty miners stood around, waiting for the shift change. Clem recognized some of the men. Bernell Holdman crushed a cigarette under his boot heel and nodded over at them, smoke coming out of his nostrils like a dragon. Orval Pullen leaned against the headframe that housed the hoisting sheaves, the pulleys that would soon be heard protesting the great loads of ore the men would dig. Elmer Schuler coughed into a handkerchief. Clem held his cap lamp against his stomach. When he moved, the early morning sunlight glanced off the Justrite's nickel plate. His was the only silvery new carbide lamp in sight. He swallowed and looked down at his boots.

"I see we got a new recruit!" Clem turned. It was a man he knew, Mr. Sawyer. The old miner squinted watery eyes at the boy. "You afeared, young Clemson?" Pap was named

Clemson; Grampy, too. Clem hoped Mr. Sawyer wouldn't call him "young Clemson" forever.

"Nope," Clem said. "I'm not afraid." His voice sounded loud and phony.

"Well, you ought to be," said Mr. Sawyer.

"Don't let Saw trouble you," Pap said. "He does enjoy himself a gruesome tale." He started walking off, leaving Clem there with the dinner pails and Old Saw.

Clem called out to him. "Pap?"

"I got to go check us in with the shift boss," Pap said. Clem watched him till he disappeared into the office.

The moment the door swung shut behind Pap, Old Saw leaned forward. Stringy gray hair hung around his white, sickly-looking face. His cheeks sank in where he was missing some teeth. A whiff of his breath made Clem figure what teeth remained were rotting in his head.

"You know, I've worked the mines all along the Ozarks Lead Belt," he said, "Fredericksburg to Bonne Terre." He had a whiny voice and a way of putting in an extra *h* sound at the start of words it didn't belong in. "Hyew" for "you," "hi" for "I," heavy on the *h* in words like *why* and *what*.

Now the old miner swept a hand back over his shoulder and then shot a bony finger northeast, past the sun. "H'all along the Lead Belt," he said again. He scratched the sandpapery gray stubble that lined his jaw and looked Clem up and down. "Boy, I got some stories that'll liketa curl your hair!"

Old Saw's were the kind of stories that had made Clem afraid of the dark in the first place.

" 'Bout four years ago, a rough colleague of mine called

Charley Underwood died a horrible death," Sawyer began. Clem glanced around again to see if anybody might be going to rescue him, but nobody was.

"Charley used to ride the shaft cage whenever it was called to the different levels of the mine. Not moments before his death, he took me and a bunch of boys on the crew down to begin our shift. We'd only gone a little ways from the shaft when we heard something. We ran back, and do you know what we saw there? Why, it's a sight I'll not soon forget."

Clem looked at him and shook his head.

"It was Charley Underwood's mess of a body. Fell two hundred feet down the shaft to his death. I'll spare you the rest." He smacked his lips, as if holding back the gory details gave him as much of a charge as telling.

Old Saw sat back and slapped his thighs. "What do you think of that? Give you a case of the heebie-jaheebies, don't it?" he cackled.

"Yessir." Clem ran a hand across his jaw.

Pap came over. "Come on," he said. "Lead Man says we're all set."

Old Saw stood up. "We'll talk more later," he said, and he pointed a bony finger at Clem before he shuffled away.

Clem felt sick. They walked over to the clean-and-change house and Pap showed Clem where to stow his dinner pail and clean clothes for later. Then they picked up their tools—pick, shovel, and sledge—and went to the elevator. He didn't want to set foot inside that cage. Eighteen or twenty of the men pressed into the cage and the shaft operator closed the door. The elevator jerked once, then began to sink. Clem looked up, and through the metalwork grille he watched the square of daylight shrink smaller and smaller and then disappear. He breathed evenly, trying to be calm against the gathering dark. He clutched his cap to his chest and he choked out a word, one small, dry whisper of prayer: "God."

Then the cage dropped with a screech, and Clem winced. He thought he could let out the scream he felt bubbling inside and nobody would hear. But he kept it in.

Now the men fired their cap lamps. Clem watched their faces change in the new, false light. Their eyes disappeared in shadow, cheek and jaw bones stood out from flesh. Pap gave Clem a nudge, and he hurried to set the cap on his head. He reached up and struck the wheel with the palm of his hand, making the sparks that fired the flame. The little wheel scraped his palm. He wondered if the soft pads of skin would harden and toughen, if he'd be numb to it one day.

And then the cage lurched and stopped, and the operator threw open the door. The men poured out, and all of them muttered something, words he couldn't quite catch. Clem moved with them. Almost instantly, the choking smell of cigarettes and something else, strong and truly foul, hit him full in the face, stopping him in his tracks.

Somebody elbowed him in the ribs. "Hey! Clem!"

It was Otto Pickens, the skinny, freckly boy he used to know from school. Now he wasn't so skinny. He looked like a man, and he was only one year older than Clem.

"I heard you was coming," Otto said. At first Clem thought he said he'd heard him screaming. He didn't want to seem scared in front of Otto. Otto shuffled out of the cage, rolling his big shoulders, and Clem followed. At school Clem knew he was better at his numbers and letters than Otto had been. But look at Otto now, the easy way he held his pick, eyes calm as fair weather. Numbers and letters don't matter in the deep dark. Clem felt himself staring, so he glanced up beyond Otto's wide shoulders. He thought he could see the tiny speck of light way up there where the shaft met daylight. He squinted to see better, and saw it wasn't anything. There was nothing up there.

Clem lowered his eyes, cleared his throat. "How you been?" he asked Otto.

"Good. Pretty good. You had about enough of school, too, then." His voice was full of knowing.

Clem looked away. "I guess."

Otto smiled. "Enough of the sun and playing ball, too, I reckon."

Clem stared at him. Maybe not all of a man yet, then. Or anyway, a man still new at it.

"Miss Pipe still giving that 'I Believe' theme?"

Clem nodded. "Just yesterday, I read mine out."

"Let's go," Pap called. Rail cars waited on the tracks to take the men to the various rock faces where they'd do the day's work of mucking ore. The same tracks would carry the ore from the rock faces back to the shaft, to be hoisted to the surface for grinding and milling.

Otto flicked the bill of Clem's cap and Clem ducked his head.

"You heard him," Otto said. They had to yell, now, over the noises of the rail car and the men. "Let's move on."

The men all climbed into waiting cars, and then the locomotive began to move, ferrying the crew along the adit tunnel.

Clem leaned to Pap's ear. "What was everybody saying?" Pap looked at him. "Back there, in the cage."

"We say '*Glückauf*,'" Pap said. "Men from the old sod brought the term, to mean 'Good luck.'" He frowned, thinking. "But more than good luck—be safe, keep your light burning." He bent toward Clem as if to share a secret, a rare glint in his eye. "And it summons the mine to open its treasures."

"Good luck and pray you don't cross the knockers," said Old Saw, intruding. Clem's shoulders crept up near his ears. He knew the old stories of the knockers and tinners, little men whose tapping might lure a miner down the wrong way, or on the other hand might lead him to a vein that was true.

Pap waved a dismissive hand. "Now, we say another thing, too. When we go on top at the end of the shift we say 'To grass,'" Pap said.

Clem swallowed hard. The thought of fresh green grass, a light breeze *shhh*ing in the branches of the silver maple in the school yard, made him long for the end of the day.

"Get a whiff of that dynamite?" Pap asked.

"A little."

"It'd best be a little," Sawyer piped up. Clem wished he'd stay out of it. "You get a noseful of dynamite fumes, and you'll get yourself a powerful headache. Happened to a fella name of Otis Minor, and he lost a day's work."

Pap ignored him. He tapped his wristwatch and lifted his eyebrows at Clem. "Three o'clock, in the a.m. and the p.m., you hear me, Clem, two times a day, they do the blasting, to break rock and free up the ore. Then they wait four hours for the gas to clear out. So you're not going to come across any fumes to speak of."

The locomotive passed by a couple of men hugging the

side of the tunnel. "And those are the roofmen," he said. "They've finished checking for loose back."

"Otherwise, a chunk might fall and liketa crush a man!" said Old Saw. He licked his lips with a quick dart of his tongue, like a lizard.

The men had to duck their heads at a few spots, or else get a crack from a support timber running crosswise. Then the car stopped and some of them got out. The men all seemed to know what to do, and where they were going to spend the shift. Clem didn't know anything, so he followed Pap. Pap would tell him how it worked.

The area they were to work was high enough to stand in and wide enough for five men, with rock columns left at regular enough intervals so the roof wouldn't collapse. The mine smelled like a hole in the ground, like dirt, until most of the men lit their cigarettes, and then Clem fairly choked on billows of smoke. And more horrible, it wasn't long before he began to gag on the stink of old, foul piss. The air in the tunnel felt cool on Clem's skin, but he was sweating. And the noise! Explosions, hammering, the *thock* of shovels, the muttering of the men and all their other bodily utterings, the clanking sound of rail cars moving constantly along the track. There was nothing about the mine that would ever change Clem's first impression: it was a busy little hell straight out of the Bible. Clem stood there and felt like he might burst into flames.

"Let's get to work, then," Pap said. And they began to muck ore. They shoveled the heavy rock and ore into big cans that got put into the underground rail cars, to be hauled up and dumped onto the grizzly and crushed and milled and the lead extracted. That was the all of it.

* * *

Hours went by. At first Clem busied himself with thoughts of Miss Pipe, and who might be sitting at his desk, and Mickey, and playing ball. When his hands stung, and he saw he'd worn a blister, he felt oddly pleased and thought about how hard he was working, like a man. But then he stopped thinking anything. His head ached, throbbing dully with the rhythm of the work: *Thock-lift-dump.*

Thock-lift-dump.

Thock-lift-dump.

After a while he realized that what was running through his mind, in time with the unrelenting *thock-lift-dump*, was a slow and measured *Hail, hail, the gang's all here.* He gave a wry smile, thinking of Linda Jean trailing monsters across the playing field, and began to whistle aloud the monotonous tune.

"It's bad luck to whistle, Clem." Startled, he glanced up. Pap was standing beside Otto, hand on his shoulder. "Now, here's a boy who makes a good miner," Pap said. Otto had three full drums lined up and waiting to be loaded onto the rail car; Clem had filled one drum. Humiliated, he turned away and his lamp lit up the earthen wall.

"It's all right," Pap said, looking into the drum. "You'll catch on and you'll naturally get stronger as you go." Clem's face burned hot, looking at Pap. Their eyes met, and what Clem saw there struck him like a fist in his gut. Expectation. Expectation he didn't think he could ever meet.

He took off one cotton glove and stabbed at his eyes to wipe out the feeling welling up. "I hate this." He spoke the words out loud. "Damn it." Once the tears began he couldn't stop them. His shoulders shook, and his heart gave two or three irregular beats, as if the living dark was taking over everything, even his blood and bones. He let out a burbling sob.

All around, the men were looking at at him, Bernell Holdman leaning on his shovel and frowning, Elmer Schuler shaking his head. Clem sniffed loudly; snot ran down over his lip and into his mouth, tasting of salt and dirt. The cotton gloves dangled off his hands like flaps of skin, and the sounds of his jagged crying filled the tunnel. Clem turned to Pap and saw the look on his face, the pinched lips. Then Pap glanced away without a word.

All the men went back to mucking. Clem dragged his sleeve across his nose and looked over where Pap and Otto worked together, their backs to him, shoulders almost touching, and he thought he'd scream with boredom and hopelessness. Nobody was paying him any attention, and so, silently, he backed away. When he came to the mouth of the tunnel they'd come in on, he turned and went into it, running twenty feet or so along the tracks.

Panting, he leaned his back against the side of the tunnel, closed his eyes, and slid down the wall, letting his legs fold, and then he sat there like a little kid wondering how long he could get away with it. With a quick movement, he reached up to his cap lamp and put out the light.

The immediate darkness was as thick as wool, pressing over his face, filling his eye sockets, wrapping down over his nose and mouth until he could scarcely breathe. His heart was pounding and he knew the dark was not filling his ear holes because he could plainly hear the blood rush and pound, and the pounding, too, of the men shoveling and the rail car pounding on the track in another dark tunnel somewhere close. He took great gulping breaths of woolen air.

Clem shot his hand up and hit his palm against the wheel to quickly fire the lamp—hiding in the dark had been a bad idea, a stupid, baby idea—and knocked the cap off the side of his head. He scrabbled on all fours like a mole till his hands found the cap, and then he stood, breathing hard, one hand holding the wall of the tunnel. Now, turned this way, he could see light from where Pap and the other men were working, and he went toward it, stumbling out of the tunnel with the confusing, sickly feeling of waking from a bad dream. He saw the figures of the men hunched over their shovels like trolls, and nobody even looked up.

Clem fired his lamp and went over to where Pap was working.

"What time is it?"

Pap set his shovel aside to study his watch. "Goin' on eleven," he said. His lamp shone in Clem's eyes, and for a moment blinded him. "We'll take a break soon. You'll see it's not so bad." Pap looked at him as if waiting for Clem to say something. His teeth glowed white in his dirty face. He waited another moment, then he clapped Clem's shoulder. "What do you say. Not so bad."

Clem breathed hard. He couldn't think of a single good thing to say about this horrible place. But he would not cry again.

"I miss the sun," he said stupidly.

"You get used to it," Pap said. He turned to Old Saw, gave him a slow wink. "Isn't that right, Sawyer." Old Saw opened his mouth, a gash in those greasy, sunken cheeks, and they laughed.

Clem made up his mind that very morning at eleven o'clock: there was no way on God's earth he was going to end up a miner.

3

HAPPY BIRTHDAY

"BLOW OUT THE candles, Clemmy!" Esther said, clapping and jumping up and down. Ma walked slowly across the small square of kitchen bearing a cake lit with thirteen candles.

"Make a wish, boy," shouted Grampy. He leaned one hand on the back of a kitchen chair, pressing the other into his lower back and bending over his small potbelly. Wrinkles fanned out across the papery skin at the corners of his eyes. Close to him, Clem thought Grampy didn't smell like the mines, he smelled like the woods, the way he figured a person should smell.

"Hang on, Dad," Pap said, "let him take a breath."

"I am hanging on!" Grampy shouted. "Only reason I'm hanging on is to get my compensation! I want what I got coming to me!"

Ma patted Grampy's bent shoulder and helped him pull out his chair to sit. "You'll get what's coming to you, old man," she said, and she kissed his freckled head when he was settled.

Then Ma waved her dish towel in the direction of the cake, and the candle flames danced. "Grampy's right, Clemson J, you best get the candles out. Do it all in one go or it's a year of bad luck. Go on, make your wish now."

A drop of hot wax made its way down a candle and puddled on the cake. Only half joking, Clem said, "I'm so bone tired I wish I'd never been born." Then he took a deep breath and he wished his real birthday wish and he blew out the candles, all thirteen.

Pap put the light on and squeezed Clem's shoulder so hard it hurt. "You'll get used to it, like I said. You'll toughen up." Clem's face went hot, picturing how he cried in the tunnel and Pap's face when he turned away. Pap looked over at Ma and nodded. "He'll learn. He'll do right fine." Clem saw in his mind Pap and Otto working side by side. He didn't want to do right fine down there in the dark. He wanted Pap to be proud of him—but for something else, anything else.

He cut a look to Esther. She smiled and touched the tip of her thumb to her temple, an old signal of understanding and sympathy between them.

Ma cut up the cake and passed a fat slice of it to Clem and a smaller slice to Esther.

"Chocolate," Ma said. "Loaded up with frosting, just how you like it."

Clem stared at the plate of dark cake on the table in front of him. "Thanks, Ma," he said. She always made him his favorite, even though Esther didn't like chocolate, but just now it didn't look good to him.

Grampy picked up his fork and dropped over his plate, giving it his full attention. He took a bite of cake and then he started to cough. Cake and gunk blew out of his mouth onto the table. Grampy's fork clattered as he pushed the plate away, even while he was still coughing into his napkin.

Clem could remember Grampy's last day on the job, a good two years before. He'd thought they might have a party then, but they hadn't. Grampy couldn't work at all, once the coughing got bad. He'd been writing letters to the St. James Lead Company, demanding compensation for loss of livelihood on account of the miners' consumption, a letter a week, every single week since. Clem had kept count of the letters at first, but then he'd stopped.

Grampy finally caught his breath and cleared his throat. "What'd you wish for, boy?" he yelled.

Clem looked at his family around the table, all of them watching him with their eyebrows lifted as if they couldn't wait to hear it. But he was so tired. His eyes slid past them and all he could see was the dark in the corner of the kitchen beyond the stone chimney, and all he could feel was the stinging in his hands where the skin was torn, and the sharp pinch of his shoulders because of digging like a woodchuck all day long beneath the crushing weight of the earth. He dropped his eyes to the crumbling chocolate cake on his plate and he thought how this was the worst, the absolute worst birthday any boy could ever have.

"I wished for a dog!"

Pap set his coffee cup down on the table with a solid thump.

"What are you yelling for?"

"I just want to be sure Grampy hears me, is all."

"Oh, he heard you. We all heard you, we have done heard you a million times, about the dog," Pap said.

"Well, why can't I get one?" Clem's voice was loud and whining, but he couldn't help it. "I hate it down there! I hate it!"

Pap pushed his plate away and stared at the table, breathing hard through his nose. Silently he held out his mug to Ma for a heat-up. She got up and got the coffee and came over and poured him some.

Pap sipped the coffee, grimaced, set down his mug, and leaned his elbows on the table. "Clemson," he said, "you got precious little time to care for a dog now." He worked his fingers together and leaned his forehead on the knot of his hands.

Clem glanced at Esther for sympathy. But Ettie wasn't listening. Her jaw had gone slack, her chest curved as if lifted by a string from the ceiling, her eyes showed the whites.

"Esther's gone," Clem said, his voice urgent but level. Everyone stopped eating and looked at Esther. They waited for the shaking to begin.

Esther had had epileptic fits ever since Clem could remember. She'd get a look in her eyes that meant she was about to go somewhere else, and then she would start to shake. It used to frighten Clem. Sometimes that would be it, she'd go away in her mind and she'd shake a bit for a few seconds, and then she'd come back. But other times, she would fall right down and shake on the ground. A fit like that would leave her sore and bruised, as if she'd been beaten. She'd been to the hospital in Bonne Terre, and even up to St. Louis on the train.

Now Esther's shoulders shot up around her ears and pulsed up and down. Her eyes rolled up and her mouth and chin worked in spasms. Then it was over. Her eyes cleared, then focused. Ma took Esther's hand and stroked it.

"You all right, lovie?"

Esther looked at her. "I think I'll lie down awhile," she said. Ma helped her scoot out the chair and walked her down the hall. The three of them left at the table watched Ma guide Esther to the back of the house, their feet shuffling, Ma murmuring soft words.

Pap sighed and his shoulders sagged. He rubbed a big hand over his face and shook his head as if to clear it, then he pointed a finger at Clem. "You see that there? That little girl, shaking and shivering? Next time you want to piss and moan about your lot, maybe you ought to give a thought to that one, huh?" His voice sounded different now. Before, he'd sounded proud to have Clem go down the mines with him, but now he sounded tired, and angry.

"Mining's what we do. We got Esther's doctor bills and we got to eat, and it's time you help out."

Ma came back in and sat at the table. "Poor little love," she said. Then, "Don't you like your cake, Clemson J?"

"It's good, Ma," Clem said, but he didn't feel like eating. It wasn't Esther's fault she was sick, he knew that. Her being sick was a terrible thing. They'd made up their special signal—the thumb to the temple, like an antler—because there was a spell where she couldn't talk, she was so sick. Of course it wasn't her fault. But, Clem figured, it wasn't the heck his fault, either.

"There's other ways of making money," he mumbled.

"What?" Grampy leaned over and yelled in Clem's ear as if Clem were the deaf one.

Pap slapped his hands flat on the table. "If you are speaking of Lewis Pitt and his kind, son, you better think again." Pap pointed a long finger at Clem, and spoke low and careful in a way that gave Clem a shiver. "Lewis Pitt is a bootlegger. Him and others like him go above the law, and they run moonshine whiskey down into Arkansas and over to St. Louis. Now, I don't say I judge a grown man taking a drink now and again. Prohibition's the work of the Bible thumpers and the politicians. But when they go and shoot a lawman over busting up a still, well that's..." he searched for a word.

Ma got up. "Nobody knows if they did it," she said.

Pap glanced at her and then looked long at Clem across the table. "You're thirteen and you're able. That's how it is." He fiddled with his fork, pressed each tine with his fingertip, and then set the fork down beside his plate.

Ma brushed a hand across the back of Clem's neck, then started stacking the cake plates. "I know you're tired today, Clemson J, and it's all new, but"—she glanced at Pap—"I understand you get used to it down there. You just do." She put another plate on the stack.

"Besides," she said, "I will not ever have a dog in this house." The fourth plate landed on the pile with a dull clack. "Not after what happened."

Clem sighed, and Pap's lips tightened into a grimace, and Grampy yelled, "What'd she say?"

Ma ignored Grampy and shook a fork at Pap. "Clem, don't you gimme that." She turned her fork on her son. "And don't you sigh and roll your eyes, Clemson J." She glared at them both, and Grampy, too. "Call me superstitious, will you?" She nodded her head. "I saw what I saw, and not a week later you know what happened."

They did know, and they knew she was going to tell it all over again. About her young widowhood, before she married Pap. About the ghost dog.

Ma had come from hill country, not to marry Pap but to marry his younger brother, Jasper. One autumn day, newly wed and pregnant, she saw a great black beast and swore it was the ghost dog, a bad omen feared by superstitious hill folk. A week later Jasper died of fever, leaving her to carry their child alone. It was later that she married Pap and gave Clem a living father.

The muscle along Pap's jaw worked, and he cleared his throat. "Lemme give you a hand with those plates."

Now Esther came back in, fair hair brushed in smooth sheets down along the sides of her face, and dressed in her floaty night dress, smiling as if nothing could ever be wrong in the world. She ran over to Clem and pressed a small, oblong box into his hand.

"Ow!" Clem showed her his blisters. He'd put some grease on them, but they stung awfully.

"Sorry," she said. "Here, let me open it for you."

Esther tore off the paper, greedy as if opening her own gift on her own birthday. She lifted the lid of the box.

"It's a pen!" she said.

Clem grinned at her. "Well, let me see it." He took it in his hands. It was a royal blue fountain pen with a silver nib. The shaft was cool and slick, the blue shot through with a darker blue, like the twilight sky the moment it thinks to go black. It was a very serious pen.

"Thank you, Ettie."

"It's from all of us," she said, "but I picked it out down to Miller's. I thought of it."

She smiled, proud of herself.

Nighttime, the two children sat on Clem's bed, one at each end.

Ettie's face glowed sickly in the bedroom light. Dark circles under her eyes looked like the remnants of a schoolyard fight.

"You look bad," Clem said.

"Gee, thanks." She forced a little laugh, and shifted on the blanket to fold one leg beneath her. "I had a fit before," she said.

"Today? Another one?"

She nodded. "On the way home from school. Don't tell."

"All right." He tapped the side of his head with his thumb to assure her.

"You'll never guess who helped me." She plucked at the blanket. "The girl with the cheek."

"Frankenstein?"

Ettie nodded. "I was going down Main Street and I felt it coming on. The next thing, I was back from it, and she was on the ground beside me, lying right down in the dirt." She resettled herself on the bed and leaned closer to Clem. "I saw the scar," she whispered. "Up close." She rocked back and tugged at the blanket again, her head tipped to one shoulder. "Clemmy?"

"Mm?"

"You ever call her Frank at school?"

Clem nodded.

"Me too. I wish't I never had."

"Me too," he said.

Esther stuck her legs out in front of her along the edge of the bed and wiggled her toes. "What did you really wish for, Clemmy?" she asked. "When you blew out your candles?"

He looked at his hands, open and blistered on his lap.

"Oh, Esther." He looked up at her. "I wished I didn't have to go back."

She sat up close. "Was it bad?"

Clem looked down at his hands again, at the broken blisters, then tugged at a bit of loose skin. It burned. He let his hands drop into his lap. "Down there, I feel like I'll die, like I'm already dead and buried."

Esther frowned. "That is very gloomy, Clemmy," she said. Suddenly her eyes got big and she clapped her hands.

"Maybe tomorrow you'll see a cardinal in a tree," she said, "and you can make your wish again for good measure."

Ma had told them about cardinals. If you see a cardinal in a tree, she'd said, you quick make a wish and throw a stone. If the bird flies up, the wish will be granted. If the bird flies downward, the wish will never come true.

"I'll keep a lookout," Clem said. "I'll wish these blisters would go away." He held out both hands to her, worn raw and shiny where the fingers met the palms. She studied his hands like a doctor, very grave.

"They do look real bad."

Otto had seen his hands earlier, at the end of the shift.

"Look at mine," he'd said, taking off his gloves to show Clem his own calluses, tough like a man's. Clem had been ashamed of his soft skin. Esther's worry, now, made him feel better. Made him feel a bit proud.

She took up his cap lamp from the crate beside his bed and fired it—took her four tries—and she put it on her head. The bill covered her eyes, and she laughed.

"I'm not supposed to waste the carbide," he said. He pulled the cap off her head and clapped out the light with his sore hand. "Pap said."

Esther stretched out at the end of Clem's bed. "Tell me a story," she said.

Clem looked up at the ceiling. He thought of wishing on a cardinal, of being in the wrong place. He thought of sleep. He looked at her, about to beg off, but she touched the tip of her thumb to the side of her face.

"Okay," Clem said, relenting. He picked up the beautiful pen she'd given him, and inspected the shaft of swirled blue.

"Once there was a very little princess who couldn't sleep, no matter what," he began.

"Oh, good goodie good," Ettie said. She shifted her shoulders, moved her legs around the other way.

Clem smiled at her maneuvers to get comfortable. She was so easy to please. He told her a story about a princess who couldn't ever sleep, no matter how many bedtime stories she was told, and a bird who couldn't ever sing, no matter how early he got up in the morning.

Clem smiled at Esther. She was just like the princess he was telling her about. She always listened to his stories. If it weren't for her, he doubted he'd even have any stories to tell in the first place. He brought the end around to the princess sleeping and the bird singing.

"The princess heard the cardinal's song. She felt a wonderful thing, and that was: peace. It would be fine, she thought for the first time, to fall asleep."

Esther frowned. "Dead?" she asked.

Clem shook his head. "Not dead," he told her. "Asleep."

"Well, you should make the story very clear about that," said Esther.

"Okay," he said, and he told the ending again. "The princess thought for the first time, it would be fine to fall asleep, and to rest, and to wake up again tomorrow and see how things look. They'll look mostly the same, the sun will come up just as it always has, but things will be a little bit different, too. That's what she heard in the bird's song."

"The end?" said Esther, yawning.

"The end."

Esther yawned again. "It's a good story. You better write it down."

She said goodnight and pulled the blanket across on the rope that split the room in two. Clem put the light out and lay down and closed his eyes. He was so tired. His shoulders ached, and his neck felt tight, as though it would crack and snap his head off if he turned wrong. He wanted to fall asleep and be numb. But he couldn't.

He punched his pillow a couple times and tried again to rest. No good. His legs and arms jumped and jerked almost as bad as Ettie's, as if he were still working, dropping the shovel, pulling it up hard, full of earth. And again. And again.

It was late, nearly midnight. He put on his cap lamp, struck the wheel and fired the light. Then he took a sheaf of paper from the crate and wrote down the story for Esther. When he was finished, he picked up *Peter Pan*. Miss Pipe had written a message in the front. He read it and winced. *May you have many thrilling adventures of your own.*

"Fire it up, Clem," Pap said the next day, on shift. They'd just come out of the elevator cage, and so far everything had gone exactly the same as yesterday—the square of daylight overhead shrinking as the hoisterman lowered the cage, the lurching stomach, the foul stench, the foreign-sounding greeting of *Glückauf*, the blackness everywhere.

Clem looked blankly at Pap. Pap jutted his chin, and his eyes were squared on a spot just over the top of Clem's head. The lamp. Clem took the cap off and slid his hand sharply along the small wheel, but it didn't fire. He tried again.

"Here, let me," Pap said. But he failed to light the lamp, too, and then Clem knew what had happened. He'd let the fuel burn out in the night, reading. He'd fallen asleep and the lamp had burned, the flame eating up all the fuel in the chamber till it was gone.

"How is it you're out of carbide already?" Pap's face was puzzled. "We filled them last night, should last a good four hours."

Clem looked up at Pap and shrugged.

Pap eyeballed Clem and passed the cap lamp back. "Well, fill it up."

Clem patted his pockets. Something was there, but not a carbide tin. He reached in and pulled out his birthday pen. It slipped from his hand and fell to the dirt; he knelt to pick it up.

Pap scowled. "You remember a pen, but forget your tin?" He took out his pocket rag, and he wiped his nose and mouth with it and then put it back in his pocket. "What're we going to do about that?"

"Well, you could fill it," Clem said.

Pap pinched his lips together and crossed his arms over his chest.

Clem felt his cheeks flush. He could picture the milk-bottle-shaped tin sitting there on the floor beside the door, full with two charges of Union Carbide, enough to last the shift. Clem put the cap on his head and he looked around. "There's enough light to see by," he said. There was a string of electric lights running along the middle of the tunnel roof, just enough that the blackness wasn't complete.

"No, Clem, you can't count on them," Pap said. "They're out as often as they're on. Down here you got to be self-reliant. You got to keep your head on straight and your light steady if something happens. It's a matter of pride. A borrower nor a lender be, says that in the Bible, or somewhere."

"Yes, Pap." It was Shakespeare, but he knew enough to keep it shut.

"You go up to the store and get yourself some more, and you'll miss your earnings while you're at it." Pap drew a hard line with his shovel and then sank the blade into the muck.

Clem started back to the elevator shaft.

"Hey. Clemmy." It was Otto. He pulled out his own hip flask, held it out to Clem. "Fill it up. I got enough, I think." He gently shook the flask. Clem hesitated.

"Go on. I bet you'll help me out some time."

"Count on it." Clem took the flask, filled the lamp base, and handed back the flask. "Thanks a lot. I'll never do *that* again."

"I know." Otto grinned. "It only takes once."

Clem slipped the pen back into his pocket and began to dig.

4

PALLY-BOY

EVEN THOUGH MA would have nothing to do with a dog, Clem had talked about a dog and longed for a dog so fiercely and for so long that he had a picture of him in his mind's eye. He'd be a bouncy, wiggly, yellow pup, with thick fur and soft brown eyes full of understanding.

The dog that showed up on a steamy day in late July was not that dog at all. A thunder and lightning storm had just passed overhead, and Grampy and Esther and Clem were sitting on the porch, pitching pebbles and waiting for the mail, when a dog came barreling over the crest of the hill.

The dog ran straight for the porch like a baseball player sprinting all out for home. Clem wondered if he should protect his sister, or duck for cover. As it came bounding closer, Clem saw it had the short, stubby legs of a beagle, the long hair of a setter, the sharp gray muzzle of a German shepherd, and the upright tail of a Lab. The dog pulled up short and stood there, panting.

The three on the porch exchanged a look, and then

studied the odd-looking dog. For his part, the dog looked around at his surroundings—the rutted porch step, the filthy mat by the door, Grampy's rocker and rickety table—and then he wagged his entire hind end. Then he made a decision by sitting firmly beside Clem. He kept sidling closer, leaning, until he was practically sitting in Clem's lap.

The dog barked loudly.

"Shhhh!" Clem wrapped his arms around the dog's neck and pressed his muzzle to his chest. "Ma's going to hear and kick your tail straight back over the hill."

The dog looked at Clem and tipped his head to one side as if listening carefully. Then he barked again. But softly.

Clem looked at Grampy, then at Ettie.

"That dog can whisper," Ettie said.

Clem scratched the dog's ears and looked up at Grampy. "You figure he's a stray?" he asked hopefully.

Grampy rubbed his stubbly chin. "Might could be," he said. "No tags, no collar, no rope on him."

"What's a good name for you, dog?" Clem wondered out loud.

Grampy offered Shep, and Esther thought of Red.

"Bandy?" said Clem, scratching one of the dog's bowed legs. Nothing seemed to Clem to meet the needs of the whole animal, he was such a piecemeal specimen. But then the dog looked up at Clem and he saw the dog's big brown eyes, and they were full of understanding. Just what he'd hoped for.

"Pal," Clem announced. "You'll be my Pally-boy, won't you." The dog thumped his tail in agreement, and Clem smiled at Esther and Grampy. "I got myself a dog!"

"Just until his rightful owner shows up to claim him," Pap said. Ma shook her head over the stove. She was stirring up a whirlpool in a pot.

"That dog don't have a rightful owner!" Grampy shouted. "No rightful owner would let a dog get so snarled up and tangly. Why, it's plain to see he ain't had a decent meal in a dog's age!" He winked at Clem.

The dog let out a single whisper-bark and everyone turned to look at him. Then, sitting up very straight, the dog pulled his lips away from his teeth and lifted his bristly brow.

"He smiled!" Ettie clapped her hands.

Grampy snorted. "More pleasant a dog I don't know if I ever saw, wouldn't you say, boy?" Grampy glanced over at Ma's back at the stove. "Fine, upright posture, soft-spoken, and a good sense of humor. Better comp'ny than plenty of people I've had the displeasure of meeting." Ma's elbow shot out pointy, stirring the pot.

Pap glared at Grampy and shook out his napkin. He glanced over at the stove, and caught a look from Ma. He sighed. "I have done said all I'm going to say on the matter," said Pap. "The dog stays only a day or two, and then he has to go."

The next day when Clem left for the mine, Pally-boy followed. Clem told him to stay, but doing what he was told didn't seem to be in the dog's nature. Clem roped him up by the lilacs, where he could crawl under the bushy branches for shade, and left him a pie pan of water and another of table scraps.

"You be good now, Pally," he said. "I'll be home here in a bit, and then we'll have some fun."

Clem looked back twice. The dog was sitting straight, watching. Clem wished he could stay with Pally-boy. But even leaving him, his heart took a little leap, just thinking about coming back up over the rise, in eight hours plus the walk time, to the welcome of Pal's funny grin. He laughed just thinking of it. He had that Christmas-morning feeling, when you unwrap your presents, and you forget about them a little bit, and then you run and check, and—sure enough—you really did get that new book or ball, and then that good, shivery, opening-a-present feeling spreads all over you again. They had to let him keep Pal, they just had to!

All morning Clem worked, mucking ore and thinking about the dog he already thought of as belonging to him.

"Isn't Pally funny, Pap?" he said.

Pap grunted.

"You heard how he knew to whisper, isn't that a good dog? Isn't he a good dog, Pap?"

"He's sure a good enough dog. A dog like that one'd make for a good companion." He looked at the tip of his shovel handle as if he was seeing something else. "Your grampy gave brother Jasper and me a bloodhound pup when I was a boy of six. Old Pitcher lived to sixteen years." He shook his shoulders a little and sniffed, yanked the shovel from the dirt. "You best not set your heart on him. Someone's bound to claim him, and even if they don't, I'm married to your mother and I plan on staying that way."

Clem watched Pap work the shovel. He was feeling about done in, with the day still stretching out ahead of him. He needed coffee. His own thermos was empty, so he took a sip from Pap's.

Oh, but it was bitter, and it burned. It seemed to scorch a hole all down his throat. It was coffee, yes, but mixed with something else.

He turned to Pap, the thermos in his hand. "What happened to Ma's coffee?"

But all of a sudden, he knew. He knew about stills hidden deep in the woods, and the rough, backwoods sorts who made the fiery stuff, and the men who ran it. Mostly, he knew from the guilty look on Pap's grim face what was in that thermos. Raw, illegal, poison-tasting moonshine whiskey.

Pap glared at Clem, and at the same time he turned a blotchy shade of red.

"Keep the dang dog!" he blurted out. He grabbed the thermos away from Clem and poured himself a level cupful. "Just keep it shut about the coffee, you hear me, Clemson?"

"Yessir!" Clem said.

"And you can wipe that smirk off your face while you're at it!"

"I wasn't either smirking!"

"You was smirking!" he said, and he stalked off.

Clem smiled. He smiled the big, dopey grin of a boy who finally got himself a dog.

"Fill in the hole again, Clemson," Pap said at supper. He set his fork on the plate and chewed. While Clem was off in the mine, Pally had dug a hole three feet deep out behind the house by the storm cellar where Ma stored canned goods and sacks of root vegetables. He'd also made a mess right at the front porch step, and Ma'd tripped in his water pan and all the laundry had tumbled out of the basket into the dirt.

"That's it?" Ma said. "That's all you mean to do about it?"

Pap swallowed. He rubbed the stubble on his chin and looked up at the ceiling where the paint was peeling. Then he bent forward over his plate and picked up his fork.

"The dog stays," he said. Ma sputtered and shot sparks at him with her eyes. Pap ducked his head, and Clem figured he was right to, Ma was firing so. But something made Clem look more carefully at Pap, the way he'd put his head down and kept it there. And he saw something he hadn't seen in a long time. Pap was smiling. He was smiling down into his plate so Ma wouldn't see. But he was smiling.

Grampy scratched Pal's ears. "Good boy!"

Pally barked happily, and pulled his lips away from his teeth.

"Quiet, Pally-boy," Clem said, just to get him to whisper-bark, which he did. Clem ate his supper with gusto. He smiled at Pap, his mouth full, busting with happiness. If Pap had granted his wish for a dog, well, it stood to reason, Clem figured, that maybe he'd grant him another wish. Clem shoveled another bite of cabbage into his mouth and smiled at Pap again.

Maybe Pap would let him get out of the mines.

5

THE WOODS

AUTUMN CAME ON. Sumac and sassafras burned red and gold against the dark green leaves of oaks and sugar maples still holding on to summer, and the long, reaching branches of the beautyberry hung heavy with candy-colored fruit.

It was Clem's day off. He clambered over a limestone boulder out by Mine Lick Creek. The woods were full of them, and the river full of stones. He and Pap had collected hundreds, lugged them out by basket and wheelbarrow, and Pap had built the rocks into a chimney in the kitchen. He'd mortared a peg in among the stones, where Ma could hang her apron. Clem grinned. Seemed like Pap was always looking for reasons to move rocks and dig dirt. The miner's life for him! Not Clem. When he read *Huckleberry Finn,* he wanted to build a raft and float away. When he read *Treasure Island,* he wanted to be a pirate. That would get him out of the mines.

Pally barked, and Clem threw a stick as far as he could through the woods where the underbrush wasn't too thick.

"Go on, Pal, fetch it!" Pally-boy ran, scaring up a pair of cedar waxwings as he went. The stick landed by a thong tree Clem had played on all his life. The trunk came up out of the ground and then made a sharp turn to the left, pointing to the creek bed, just the way the Indians trained it to grow a long time ago, to mark the good water of a spring.

Pally took the stick in his teeth, and wrapped his big grin around it.

"Good boy! Now bring it on back!"

Pal stared at Clem, blinking and winking. A breeze brushed his ruddy fur up like a milkweed burst, and he turned and trotted off with the stick.

"Aw, Pally-boy! You're supposed to fetch it back!"

Clem followed, climbing over the thong tree and going deeper into the redbuds and dogwoods, long past flower now, and down into the creek bed, seeping with cool water.

"Pal? Pally-boy, where'd you go?" Clem's voice rang against the stones of the creek bed. He began to walk again, his canvas sneakers moving heavily in the stream. He slipped on a rock and nearly fell all the way in.

Clem heard an answering bark but it was muffled and far off. He followed the sound where the creek bed briefly narrowed, ducking under limbs and scratching against the pricker brush. Pal's bark came again. Clem went around a twist in the waterway, and deeper into the hollow.

He stopped and stood still to listen, letting his heart slow. The wind had come up a little, and dark had come down around without him noticing it fall. This kind of dark wasn't complete, like the mines, and Clem wasn't afraid, exactly, not yet. Still, he always carried a flashlight and a pack of saltine crackers, just in case, and now he took the flashlight out of his rucksack.

"Pally?" he called into the blowing air. A twig snapped and he turned sharply to the sound. Panther? He shone his flashlight and looked all around, breathing hard.

The bubbling water in the creek bed, normally such a cheerful chatter, sounded louder now. Something went plop close by and Clem jumped. Probably a frog.

Then he heard a strange sound, a sound like nothing natural he'd ever heard before in the woods. A *thump-thump-thump*. He tried to make it the knocking of a woodhen. He listened. *Thump-thump-thump* came again. No. More of a rumbling thump than a knocking thump. And then the smell of burning. And something else, like Ma's bread dough rising, but sour. The thumping noise came at regular intervals, about every ten seconds. His heart pounded, too, as he walked toward the noise. What could be making such a racket? In the darkness now, he crept along the creek and around another twist in the stream. And then he saw something strange. He cut his flashlight, dropped down, and hid behind a bush.

A lantern lit up the dark shapes before him. A big black tank, like a woodstove, squatted in the middle of a level spot along the creek. A pipe sprouted out of it and led to a couple of big wooden iron-ring barrels, with pipes connecting the lot. Smoke and steam chugged into the air above the contraption, as if it had its own weather system. Off to one side of this setup was a canvas cot with a heap of blanket.

Clem looked all around in the dark. Nobody there. But the heap of blanket, the thumping, the lit lantern all told him someone had just left and might be back any minute. He crept closer, very quiet.

A coiled sort of a business jutted out of one drum and dripped into an earthen jug. Several more jugs just like it were lined up nearby. *Thump-thump-thump*—again he jumped. He knew what this was. It was a moonshine still.

Now he stood very close to the black barrels. He reached out one finger and touched the end of the copper piping where the liquid dripped out. He licked his fingertip. Then he picked up the jug and sipped from it, burning his lips and throat, all the way down to his gut.

A sound. He set down the jug and crawled on hands and knees into the underbrush, heart pounding, breathing in gulps. A man stepped into the clearing, picked up the jug at the end of the piping and peered into it, then put another one down. He turned. A blaze of lantern light fell across his face, all yellow planes and black hollows. A serviceman's-issue cap shadowed the eyes. A long, droopy mustache dragged down the sides of his mouth.

The man grunted and stood, and set the jug he'd taken up over by a tree, where now Clem saw there were several other jugs. A rifle leaned up against the tree.

Now a second figure came into the clearing. A girl. She turned and stepped into the light of the lantern. Dark hair hung down, covering half her face. A tattered dress barely reached her knees, which were bare. She shook her hair back and Clem saw the awful scar. It was the girl from school, the one they called Frankenstein. Clem thought of how she'd helped Ettie when no one else was around. Linda Jean.

Something went *snap*, followed by a brushy sound. The

man's head whipped around. He spoke to the girl and in a flash his arm reached for the rifle. Clem gasped and stared into the woods, his heart hammering. It wasn't a panther. Pal's pointy snout shone in the half-light, sniffing.

The moonshine man pulled the gun to his shoulder and sighted along the barrel, aiming into the wood on the other side of the creek from where Clem hid. "Who's there?" he called out, his voice low and ragged. Linda Jean moved behind the tree. Moonshine jerked his head side to side, thrusting the rifle into the air in front of him and craning to see what was up there.

And then all hell broke loose. Pally came bounding down the bank. The man shouted and took aim. Clem scrambled on all fours up from his hiding spot shouting, "Don't shoot! Pal! Pally-boy, no! Don't shoot!"

Moonshine turned his head and his gun on Clem. "Who's there?" he shouted, and in the next instant Pally-boy leaped at the man and hit him dead center and knocked him down and—*bang!*—the gun went off. Pally sank his teeth into Moonshine's leg, and the man screamed bloody murder.

Then Pal was racing to Clem at top speed and Clem turned and ran, the two of them crashing through the woods, and the screams of the man and the *thump-thump-thump* of the still rang and pulsed against the river rocks, and Clem's feet pounded and his heart hammered and the screams followed the boy and the dog all the way out of the hollow.

They lost him. He couldn't have run far with Pally's teeth marks burning holes in his leg. Clem pictured Moonshine

Man pouring a stream of the alcohol over the wound and grimacing under his thick mustache. Did the girl—Linda Jean—did she dress the wounds? Was she his daughter? One of the stories he'd heard about the strange, silent girl was that she got the scar in an explosion in the woods. Had it been a still that blew up? Had she seen Clem sipping from the jug?

Clem was relieved to come upon the thong tree, finally, a landmark he could recognize even in the moonlit dark. He'd dropped his flashlight and the soda crackers. Clem sat on the bench in the trunk and waited for his heart to slow down. Pal panted and dripped from his mouth. He rubbed his snout on Clem's thigh, and Clem smoothed his hands over the dog's head. "Good boy, good dog."

Pal went and picked up a stick in his teeth. He cocked his head. He winked.

"Are you putting me on, Pally-boy?" Clem said. He was still shaking. But Pally looked so fine and friendly, as if he hadn't just run at a man with a rifle pointed at him and saved Clem's life. He owed Pal a game of fetch if that was what the dog wanted. Clem took the stick and he threw it. Pal chased into the trees, and a moment later came trotting back. He dropped the stick at Clem's feet, and pulled his lips back in a grin.

"That's the idea, Pal," Clem said. His hand quivered as he stroked the velvet ears. He'd gotten used to the smell of damp fur, and the sound of the dog's snuffs and sneezes and snorts. The black, rubbery gums. The dry, cracked round pads on the bottom of the dog's feet, and the strange smell of the paws, the smell he finally identified as warm saltines.

"Good dog," he said.

* * *

He slept badly.

Moonshine's oath kept screaming in his head. "I'll find you!" he yelled when they ran away and left him bleeding in the woods. "I'll kill you and the damn dog! I'll kill your kin!"

But it wasn't Moonshine's threat that had kept Clem quiet at the supper table that night and kept him from sleep. He knew what he should have done when he'd come upon the still. He should have hightailed it out of there. But he hadn't. He'd crept up close and tasted of it. And with the moonshine burning in his mouth, he'd thought of what that taste meant. Money. He'd thought of running away into the woods, running away from Pap and the mines, and sickly Esther, and Ma and her hill-folk superstitions, and Grampy's hacking cough, his lungs full up with silica dust. Running away to money.

Lying in his bed, Clem saw himself moving along the ground like a weasel to that still. For a white-hot minute, he was ashamed to remember now, he'd wanted the pirate's life.

6

LINDY

FIVE DAYS ON straight shift, Clem could barely utter the miner's greeting or farewell, but he was obligated to, for luck. *To grass* sounded tight in his mouth, a voice that meant he was trying to be brave. He hated that voice. Finally his day off came again, and he busted free with Pally-boy. He'd felt as if he'd never get out of doors again, and he was filled with gladness to be out in the woods and free.

"To grass!" he shouted to the sky, his voice just the one for a boy and his dog.

Clem threw a stick for Pally, who crashed through the underbrush after it. When he didn't come right back, Clem's cheeks went cold, remembering the last time Pal had run off in the woods and disappeared, and how they'd met up in the sights of Moonshine's gun. He shook it off. They were far from the still on Mine Lick Creek.

Clem heard a bark, but it was soft, like one of Pal's whisper-barks. He followed it along a rocky outcropping till he heard the soft bark again. This time it seemed as if it was coming from beneath his feet. He scrambled down and ducked under the limestone shelf, pulling away the bunched vines that draped over the rock face. Behind the twisty curtain was a hole about the size of a kitchen cupboard.

"Pal?" Clem called. His voice sounded strangely loud. No answer except the sighing and whispering of wind against rock, and water dripping a regular beat. He shuddered.

Then Pally came barreling out of the hole. When he saw Clem, his lips pulled back from his teeth in his doggy smile, eyes bright. He wagged all over, then spun around and waited, completely still, watching the hole. And then a head covered over with black hair poked out of the cave entrance. Pally leaped with all four paws in the air, and Clem jumped back, heart pounding in anticipation of a wolverine or some other creature. But it wasn't an animal coming out of the hole. It was a person.

It was that girl again, Franken—Linda Jean!

Linda Jean dusted her hands on her dress and looked from Pally-boy to Clem.

"I don't know who's more of a scaredy-cat," she said. "Your crazy-looking mutt, or you."

Clem stared at her, loose-jawed with surprise. He'd never heard her speak before. She darted her hand to her face and smoothed her black hair over her cheek. But Clem had gotten a look. The wrong words came to his mind: bubbled Yorkshire pudding, veined cabbage leaf, molded clay, leather.

He sensed he'd kept his eyes on her face a moment too long. He jerked his head and looked at Pally-boy instead.

"He wasn't afeared that time, though, when he bit my daddy." Linda Jean pointed hard at Pally-boy. Pally cocked his head at her and answered. *Yip! Yip-yip!*

"He was about to kill us!" Clem took a step toward Pally and put his hand protectively on the dog's head. "Pally only was doing what he had to do." Clem's other hand, at his side, made a fist. He was prepared to fight Linda Jean, even if she was a girl.

Linda Jean's face split into a grin. Another first for Clem, seeing the girl smile.

"What's so funny?" he asked her. He was still ready to fight, but a little scared of her. He'd heard another story that she'd got that awful scar in a fistfight with a grown man.

"You," she said. "Ha! If you hadn't run off I'd of thanked you that night. He was all right. He was sore. But he howled like a baby, and it did my heart glad, I can tell you that. Sometimes I got to skip school for it, to work for him. Other times it's nights, all night long sometimes, here or there."

Clem's hands relaxed. It looked like he wasn't going to have to fight her after all. "Your ma doesn't have anything to say about it?"

She shook her head, hair swinging wildly side to side. She crossed her arms over her chest and stood there looking stubborn and frowning, the way she did at school.

Clem tried to read her silence. "You don't have a ma?"

"I do too have a ma," she said, thrusting her arms firmly down her sides and leaning toward him. She rocked back on her heels and drew her hair down over the scar again. "She went away, is all." Her glance cut left, and she worked her lips between her teeth.

"She paints. Landscape pictures. And she has to travel to all kinds of pretty places so she can do her work. But she's coming back for me, I know that much."

"When?"

"Well, she didn't give me an exact time, Mister Tick-Tock-Clock," she said, stuffing her hands into the patch pockets of her filthy dress. "But she promised." She pulled out a small folded square of white cloth from her pocket. "I carry her hankie, see?" It was pretty, with embroidered flowers and letters, and cleaner than anything else on her person. She folded it again and replaced it in the pocket. "I'll give it over when she comes back. She'll know who I am, then. She'll know it's me when I give it. It's been a bit since I seen her...." Her hand smoothed the black curtain of hair over her cheek once again, and she glanced at Clem, something complicated in her face, a mix of defiance and fear. "I look different now. She'll know me by the hankie."

Clem was still for a moment. He moved his hand in the air between his face and hers, and peered at her face, as if to see around the black curtain of hair. "How'd you get it?"

"None of your dang business, nosy-pants!" she said.

Clem drew back. "You're the one brought it up!" he said. "I don't care, not hardly. I was just asking. I was just being polite."

There was a silence.

"Dog bite," she said, glaring first at Clem, then at Pally-boy.

Dog bite wasn't one of the stories Clem had heard before. He doubted this story was any more true than the others. She was a liar, that much was for sure.

Suddenly Linda Jean tugged the hair aside and shoved her face toward Clem. "There, you happy?"

Clem looked away. "Sorry," he mumbled. He didn't know what he was apologizing for, but it seemed like what he should do. Still—the scar, the drunken daddy, the working all night, the ma gone away. He did feel sorry for her. He figured she had it even tougher than he did. He looked at her and tried a smile. She didn't exactly smile back, but her glare seemed to soften.

"You want to do something?" he said.

She looked at him and frowned. Then she shrugged. "I would, but I got to go to work," she said. Her smile was sly. "You ever hear of the Bell Tree?" she said.

Clem shook his head.

Linda Jean started walking, and Clem and Pally fell in beside her. "Well, you won't hear about it from me, then, neither. It's my place of employment, so to say, the Bell Tree. I bet you walked by it a million times and never knowed it was there."

"Real work? Work for money?" Clem was interested.

She nodded. "Sure, real money."

"If you're making all that money, how come your dress is so raggedy?"

She stopped and put her hands on her hips. "I don't care two shakes about dresses. I'm saving it. I'm saving it secret, where my daddy don't even know. When my ma comes for me, I'll be ready." She started to walk again.

Clem tugged on her sleeve. "Tell me what the Bell Tree is, Linda Jean," he said. Pally-boy danced around her, nipping the air.

She jerked her shoulder to pull her arm away. "I'm not telling." She began to walk again. "And it's Lindy." He looked at her. "Teacher calls me Linda Jean, but I go by Lindy."

"Okay."

"You're not at school anymore," she said.

"No."

"I hate all them fancies at school, always staring and whispering. They call me Frank. For Frankenstein. You ever hear them call me that?"

He felt his face flush. "Maybe they don't talk about you as much as you think."

"Mostly it's the girls. I hate girls. I hate school."

"I love school. I miss it."

"Why'd you quit?"

"I didn't quit," he said, his voice loud. "I had to."

She didn't say anything. They walked on through the trees, the sun making shadows of leaves dance on the floor of the woods. Pally pounced on a shadow; finding nothing trapped in his paws, he howled in dismay. Clem and Lindy laughed. And then, as they walked together in the quiet, Clem told her about the mine, about the darkness and the blisters and the stink. About Grampy's hacking cough. About Old Saw's awful stories. It felt good to talk, to get it all out. He knew it was partly relief from having somebody listen to him; he couldn't talk to Esther, not about the dark things.

"You know about my sister, Esther? You helped her one time. She told me."

Lindy nodded. "I seen her with the fits. I didn't know but she might be dying. So I got down next to her and I cleared away the rocks and so on. I seen you care for her."

"Thank you for that," Clem said.

She shrugged. "It wasn't anything." But her lips turned at the corners, a bit of a smile.

"I'd do anything to get out of the mines," Clem said.

"You want out so bad, you ought to dig to China." Lindy made a shoveling motion with her hands. "Dig a hole, maybe you'll come out the other side of the world."

"I need money." Clem touched her shoulder. "Lindy, if there's something, some work I can do that makes real money, I want to do it."

They'd come to a large pin oak. Lindy glanced at it and stopped. "All right." She looked at him. "Clem," she said, using his name for the first time. Clem felt a funny movement in his chest at the sound of his name in her mouth. It surprised him.

"All right," she said again. "I'll never be rich, so it doesn't make much difference if I split it with you. You could work the Bell Tree with me any old time."

Clem looked seriously at her. "Does it have to do with moonshining?"

She nodded. "It does. Folks come there, a place well out the way where they won't be seen, and they sneak a drink."

"My pap would kill me," Clem said, "if yours didn't first." He rubbed Pally's neck.

"Aw, he wouldn't even know that dog's the same one bit him. Drunk off his head. I told him it was a bear that night, just to fun him."

Pally gave Lindy his smile, and she laughed. Not a rough sound this time, but a nice laugh, high and sweet.

"Even so, might as well avoid him, my daddy. He can be right mean," she said. She fingered the cloth of her dress. "Come tomorrow. He's going to be gone, running with Lewis Pitt down to Annapolis."

"I can't. I've got a shift." His stomach went queasy.

Lindy shrugged. "Suit yourself."

Clem looked at her and swallowed. No way could he skip out on his shift. No way, no how.

"Maybe sometime," he said.

She nodded and then looked at the sun, marking its position in the sky above the big pin oak. "I make it about ten o'clock," she said. "That's when we put out the bell." Lindy looked over her shoulder. "You best go now." She turned back and pushed him, her small hands pressing briefly where the bones of his rib cage met in the center of his chest. He stepped backward.

"See you around, then," he said.

"Okay, then." She turned and disappeared behind the pin oak tree.

"Come on Pally-boy," Clem said, heading away toward town. Behind him in the woods, a bell tinkled, soft and high, like Lindy's laugh.

7

TREASURES

WHEN CLEM CAME home from his shift the next day, Grampy was reading the newspaper and Ma was attacking an onion. The sharp smell filled his nose and stung his eyes. He passed through the kitchen without stopping. Pal trotted beside him, even though the dog wasn't often allowed in the house. If Ma didn't see him, Clem would smuggle him in and he'd go under Clem's bed and stay there, quiet as a mouse. Most times, she would sniff him out and level a spoon at him, or a butcher knife or a carrot or whatever she had handy to point with, and say one word: *Out.* But Ma didn't happen to see him this time, or smell him, and they walked on through, with only a wink from Grampy.

"Get Ettie for me and come help get supper on," Ma called without turning from the onion.

Clem went into the back room and pulled aside the blanket curtain. Esther was sitting cross-legged on her cot, curled over, poking through the treasure chest she kept. The chest was about as big as a bread box, quartersawn oak stained dark, a tiny key on a thin pink ribbon always in the lock. Sometimes she hid the box, and Clem wondered if she wished she could have some privacy, or if she had secrets she kept from him.

"Ma wants us in the kitchen."

She looked up. "Remember this one, Clemmy?" She held out a small stone.

Clem stepped over and took the stone, warm from Esther's hand, and rubbed it with his thumb. He remembered. He'd been walking in Mine Lick Creek up to his ankles, poking around the river bottom for mussel shells to sell for making buttons. At first he thought the rock was actual jewelry, because of the way it flashed and winked in the clear, moving water. It was the perfect shape of a heart.

Clem handed the stone back to Esther and she turned it over one more time and set it back in the box. "It's one of my best treasures," she said. "Treasure number seven." The entire collection—stones, a blue-green feather, pressed flowers, a scrap of red foil gift-wrap—it was all accounted. She liked heart-shaped things especially.

Pally-boy started to whine and pace around the room. "Hey, Pally," Clem said, "calm yourself, Ma didn't see you," and he scratched his ears. The dog quit pacing and stood by, but his ears were up and forward, on alert.

"Ettie, we better help or she'll come in here and wave her knife around." Clem scratched Pal's ears again. "Isn't that right, Pally-boy? You stay here, Pally. You stay." Pal pawed the floor like a horse and whined. "It's all right, Pally," Clem told him.

Clem left Esther putting the treasures back into the box and headed to the kitchen. "Be right there," she called.

In the kitchen, Clem reached up high for the plates in the cupboard and then he heard it. Pally's yelp. He froze, and his armpits prickled. Ma set the knife down on the butcher block and sighed, then turned to Clem with one hand on her hip. She leveled a long look at him through narrowed eyes. "Clemson J, what have I told you about that dog in this house?"

He lowered the plates and was thinking up some kind of answer to give her when Pally spoke again—a loud and serious barking from low in his throat. Clem hadn't ever heard such a low sound from Pally, not even when he was biting Moonshine. He set the plates down on the counter.

"What's all the hubbub, bub?" Grampy shouted.

"You put him out this minute," Ma said.

"Pally! Stop that, Pally!" Clem went to the back room. Pally was pacing and prancing up and down alongside Ettie's cot, his paws trampling bits of rock and red foil and pressed flowers. Esther's treasures littered the floor. Pally turned his head to Clem, and his furious bark rose to an urgent whine: Ettie was having a fit.

Her neck and back arched up off the cot as if she'd been charged with electricity. The cot jerked and bounced off the floor and against the wall. The knuckles of her right hand banged against the floorboards, her left arm ran up the wall, and it waved and knocked there like the mast of a ship in a storm. Her face was twisted and bluish. White spittle collected at the corners of her gaping mouth and her eyes rolled back in her head, showing the whites. She was making a soft wet choking sound.

"Ma! Ma!" Clem leaped to Ettie. He turned her head to one side and stuck his fingers into the back of her mouth.

Her tongue was slippery and fat. But it looked as if she was choking, and he had to get her tongue out. She gagged. Clem was afraid he was going to kill her. But then she took a big breath. Ma ran in, and he stepped back. Esther's jerking body slowed, and then it was over.

"Get some water," Ma said. Clem ran to the pump and filled a tin cup.

When he ran back into the room, Clem saw Esther was breathing again. Ma smoothed Ettie's pale damp hair off her forehead, where it was tangled and stringy with sweat, and patted her over and over again, humming something with no tune.

Esther's eyes were closed and she was resting peacefully. Pally put his nose in Clem's hand and whined, as if to ask, "Is Ettie okay?"

Ma turned and pointed the tin cup at Pally. "Out," she said.

Clem knelt and put his arms around the dog. "If it wasn't for Pally, we might not have known! Ettie was going to choke, Ma!" He buried his nose in Pally-boy's red-brown neck and breathed in deep. He smelled of dirt, and a little sour, and Clem vowed he'd give him a good scrubbing tomorrow.

Ma stared at Pal and then she lowered the cup and fiddled with the handle.

"Go and give him a walk," she said. "I'll set the supper table."

Clem watched Pap scratching Pally's ears in the kitchen and speaking gently to him, and a new assurance pulsed through his veins and made him stand up straighter. Pally-boy. What a good dog, and Pap knew it!

"You love him, too, don't you, Pap," Clem said.

Pap grunted.

"I'd sure like to spend more time with him!" Clem said hopefully.

Pap nodded. "He's a fine dog, Clem. He sure is fine."

Later, through the screen door, Clem saw Ma standing on the porch, the soft light of dusk touching the tips of her hair and turning it gold. She knelt, holding her plate in front of her like the church offering, and she scraped most of her own supper into Pally's bowl. Pally trotted up onto the porch to investigate the dish. She held her hand flat above his back as if wondering the right way to touch a dog, and then she went and patted him thoroughly. She stroked his head, as tenderly as she'd stroked Esther's hair, and then each ear, and Clem could hear Pal's gentle snufflings and a single murmur. "Good boy." Finally she stood and came in carrying her empty plate. She looked at Clem and then away, and waved the plate like a tambourine.

"Well," she said, "I wasn't much hungry."

8

A CAVE PEARL

WITH ESTHER GOING through a bad spell, Clem went to see Miss Pipe at school on his day off to ask her for a book Esther might like. "A girl book," he told her.

Miss Pipe smiled at that, and handed him *Alice in Wonderland*.

"For a girl book, it's pretty good," she said. "I trust you're finding time to read as well, Clem?"

"Some," Clem said. "I'm pretty worn out, though, and half the time I just fall asleep with the book open." He looked around the classroom. "Mining doesn't leave you too much time for reading or anything."

Miss Pipe leaned to pull down a wooden seat, hinged, as all the seats were, from the wrought-iron legs of the desk behind it. "Sit," she said. She pulled down a seat for herself beside him.

"You know, where I come from, there are lots of different types of work. I went to college in New York City, and then when I graduated I looked for work as a teacher, and I answered the advertisement in the newspaper and out I came to Leadanna on the train. In the city there are people who write articles and stories for the papers and periodicals, and there are publishing houses, Clem, and architectural firms, and all kinds of things. You'd be amazed. You should see all the buildings going up!"

Clem sat on his hands, hunching his shoulders. "I could be a builder, I guess." Even to his own ear his voice sounded sullen, and he didn't quite know why. He used to like how she would hint that he might be someone special. But now it seemed unfair of his teacher to tell him about other ways there were to be in the world, when he couldn't even go to school anymore.

"You could be an architect." Miss Pipe smiled, but a knot drew up between her eyes. "Ten miles from here there are people who are not the slightest bit aware of the American B mine, if you can believe it."

"I can't, hardly," Clem said. "Mining's everything."

"Here it's everything," Miss Pipe said, "but I assure you there is a wide world out there beyond the St. Francois Mountains, or across the Mississippi." Miss Pipe stood abruptly. She pointed at the window, her arm fixed as a compass arrow. "Look out there, Clem," she said. "If you were to walk to the top of Goggin Mountain, right now, you would see paths leading in all directions—Chicago, New York." She looked at him brightly. "Clem, what I'm talking about is—possibility."

Clem looked at his boots. He'd hosed them off in the clean-and-change house, but they still showed the dirt. He thought of Esther at home in her bed, and Grampy coughing out on the porch in his chair, rocking endlessly. Chicago? New York City?

"Might as well be Oz, or Neverland," he said, and immediately wished he hadn't.

Miss Pipe raised her eyebrows at Clem and then she flushed all at once, snapped the book closed, and patted her hair.

"Tom," she said.

Clem shifted in his seat and saw a tall man holding his hat in both hands. His forehead was pale white where the hat normally sat, and the skin below his eyebrows and on his hands was tanned brown from sun and weather. A farmer, like his own daddy'd been.

Clem remembered the story of his real father, Jasper. Ma had come from hill country, where people never went much beyond their own front door, on their own land, their entire lives. Ma'd come from away around the other side of Goggin Mountain to marry Pap's brother.

"Jasper was the better-looking of the two," Grampy had told Clem at the top of his lungs. When Jasper died not four months after, Pap took her in, pregnant and sick with sorrow, and they'd married. Grampy was the only one who ever talked about Jasper.

"Jasper was different; he wasn't ever going to be a miner like his old man and his brother, no sir." Grampy shook his head. "Nope, he was a farmer, that one, even though there was not one single sign that it was ever going to work out for him. Still, he was a stick-to-'er, that's for sure." Grampy looked at Clem. "Your ma about died of heartache, for a while there, when he passed. But it wasn't too long before she saw what had to be done, and agreed to marry Clem. Of course she gave Jasper as your middle name, after him.

And your Christian name, Clemson, for your Pap, a'course, on account of gratitude. Didn't set too well with him." Grampy rocked back and forth. "Still, they done all right."

"Mr. Gibson," Miss Pipe said now, "this is my student— my former student—Clemson Harding." The man stepped forward and stuck out his hand, and Clem stood and took it. "Clem, I'd like you to meet Mr. Tom Gibson."

Clem pretended he was shaking hands with his real daddy. He wished he'd known him. If he were alive, Clem could be a farmer, too. Maybe his real daddy would have let him do something else altogether. Still, he thought, smiling at Mr. Gibson, it seemed like Pap was coming around.

Miss Pipe gave Clem the book and said good-bye, and Clem watched his teacher and the farmer walk away. Just past the big maple on the school grounds, he saw Miss Pipe slip her hand into the crook of Mr. Tom Gibson's elbow.

"Down, down, down," Clem read to Esther. " 'I wonder how many miles I have fallen?' said Alice. 'I must surely be somewhere near the center of the earth by now. Perhaps I shall fall right through.'" He paused. He could picture the scene easily, the light of day closing to a pinprick away above Alice's head, and the darkness swallowing her up.

Esther touched the back of Clem's hand. He turned to her. She was wearing her good blue linsey-woolsey.

"Is that what it's like?" Esther asked, looking hard at him. She fingered the blue velvet trim of the dress. "In the mine, I mean? Like you must be down, down, down near the center of the earth?"

"Well, you don't pass by any cozy bookshelves on the way down, the way Alice does, I can tell you."

He found his place again. "Alice wondered sadly how she was ever going to get out again." Clem's eyes smarted, and he put the book down and pressed his fingers against his eyelids.

"I'm sorry, Clemmy," Esther said.

Clem's fingers made a teepee over his nose, and then he sniffed and dropped his hands to his lap. He looked at Esther. She'd slid down her pillows and sat at the bottom, slumped and puny-looking in her bed. She was still exhausted from her recent fit. She spent so much time in bed. Sometimes, he knew, she put on her best dress just to feel as though she might be going somewhere special later. Sometimes she'd sleep in that dress, with the velvet trim. She said it gave her interesting dreams.

"Do you wonder sadly, too?" Clem said. She raised her eyes to meet his. Of course she wondered sadly how she'd ever get out again. Stupid question.

"How about a story?" Ettie asked. "One of yours."

Clem closed the book and set it on the bed beside him. He thought about a story Old Saw had told him, about a drillman who drowned in mud. But he didn't want to give Ettie the kind of nightmares Old Saw gave him.

"Did I ever tell you about the boy who got rich?"

Esther shook her head. She looked so tired.

"Well, there was a boy from near here, just over in Reynolds County, and this wasn't very long ago, either. He was out one day tramping through the woods on his way fishing for crappie, when all of a sudden his hair stood straight up on end and he dropped his fishing pole and looked around. Something caught his eye, some movement behind a red-bud, and slowly, slowly, he crept over that way."

Clem cleared his throat and Ettie pulled her sheet up under her chin.

"He wasn't afraid, not really, because here was a boy who wasn't afraid of anything."

"Grampy says a little fear is good," Esther said, "and a lot of fear turns you to stone and you might as well be dead."

"Right. So he goes behind the tree and there he sees a pretty scary thing. He sees a ghost dog, eight feet long, black as pitch."

"Like Ma's!" Ettie said.

"That's right, just like Ma's. Only instead of running away like Ma did, this boy, I forget his name so we'll call him Clem"—Esther smiled at that—"Clem followed that ghost dog close as he could.

"Before long, the ghost dog led him to a hole in the side of old Taum Sauk."

Esther sat up. "I thought you said Reynolds County."

"He started out in Reynolds County, but he followed the dog a long way, all afternoon, and they crossed county lines. Okay?"

She sat back. "Okay."

"So when they got to the cave in Taum Sauk, the ghost dog raised his muzzle and he howled, and then he turned his big shaggy head to Clem and he nodded one time like this." He nodded his head, up, down, and Ettie copied. "And then the ghost dog disappeared into the hole."

"But like I said, instead of running away scared, this boy—this boy went right on in, into the dark. He couldn't see a thing, and he didn't have a lamp. He listened. He could hear the kind of sounds water makes—gurgling, seeping, drip-drip-dripping. And now he could see. The cave had gone gray, or his eyes had got used to the dark. He saw hundreds of stalactites hanging from the roof of the cave, and water dripped slowly from the tip of each one, into pools of water below. And then he felt the ghost dog right beside him. He stood as tall as the boy, and smelled of smoke. The ghost dog lowered his head and drank from the water. Then he looked at the boy and Clem understood he was supposed to drink from the water, too. So he did. He knelt and he put his face in the little pool beneath a huge stalactite, and drank deep."

Clem looked all around, trying to think what could happen next. He saw the moon out the window, hanging perfect and round in the black sky.

"And when he stopped drinking there was something in his mouth. He stuck his fingers in between his teeth and you know what he pulled out?"

Esther shook her head.

"It was a cave pearl. Round and bright as the moon, and big, a half inch across. The minerals made the pearl, over years and years and more years dripping off that stalactite into the pool. And the ghost dog had showed Clem the way to it."

"There isn't any such thing as a cave pearl, is there?" Ettie wanted to know.

"There is," Clem said, "Grampy told me."

"Well, what happened then?"

Clem paused; he didn't know what to say next. He didn't know how to round up this story to make Esther happy. He wanted to give her something light and optimistic, not dark and gloomy like Old Saw's stories.

"Well, I wondered, too, what happened," he said slowly. "And so I asked about that boy, and I found out he took the pearl and he sold it in Chicago and made a lot of money, and he never got sick, and he never had to work another day in his life."

Esther stared at Clem and her eyes narrowed. She made a *humph* sound and crossed her arms over her chest.

"What?" he said.

"It's just it's not a very good ending."

"What's not good about it? He never gets sick, he never has to work?" Clem looked down at the book on the cot beside him and shrugged. "That's a darn good ending."

"I guess," she said. She laid her head back on the pillowcase and looked up at the ceiling. Her hands started waving slowly in front of her face. "How about he gives the cave pearl away to someone who needs it, an old, sick hag everybody thinks is a witch, and it turns out that the witch is really a princess, and all it takes to break the spell on her is a gift by surprise. And—poof!"—her hands splayed as if to sprinkle fairy dust—"she turns into a princess and Clem and her sail away to her country, where they live happily to this day."

She turned her head to the side on her pillow and smiled at Clem.

"Okay," Clem said. "That's good."

Esther nodded, satisfied, and turned her head to rest more comfortably.

When he thought Esther was asleep, Clem carefully got up off her cot, leaving Pally-boy beside her, keeping watch.

Without opening her eyes, Esther lifted one hand, pinched pointer finger and thumb together, and moved her hand across the air. "Write that story down," she said.

9

A THING OF BEAUTY

ABOUT MIDDAY, ON shift with Pap, Clem came across a piece of rock too large to shovel. He chopped at it with his pick to break it up, and when it cracked apart, his lamp shone on something impossibly sparkly. He gasped and looked around.

At break, Clem took the strange rock up to the light and looked at it more carefully in the sun. Clear purple and pink built up around a core, all crusted over on the outside. It looked to him like the riches of some goblin king, buried in the middle of the mine, and Clem wondered if a knocker had led him to it. Had he heard a tiny tapping, before he hit the crystal? He thought of Esther. How she'd love this for her treasure chest. It wouldn't even fit into it!

Pap's low voice dragged Clem's mind back. Pap leaned heavily on his sledge like an old man with a cane. "Don't you go writing a poem about it."

Old Saw dropped half a pasty into his dinner pail and shuffled over to see.

"Why, it's a crystal," Sawyer said. "I knew a fella, name

of Ernest Walters, found one of them one time, down in Colorado. I don't know if this is the same sort, but that fella's crystal was worth quite a lot of money!"

By now several men were gathered, and Clem was feeling like a famous person. Otto patted him on the shoulder. The mining engineer and the shift boss walked over and looked at the crystal.

"It's a nice one," said the engineer, Mr. Weiler. "Fluorite."

"Mm-hm, boy!" The boss shook his head. "Now that is a thing of beauty, ain't it?" Mr. Forsythe looked at Clem and smiled, but not, Clem thought, with his eyes. His gaze cut to Pap, but he spoke again to Clem.

"You find this, boy?"

Pap's head sank in between his shoulders, his arms ramrods on the sledge.

"Yessir!" Clem said. "I found it myself this morning, and I thought it might be something." Clem was talking too much, he knew, and beaming foolishly, but he couldn't help it.

Mr. Forsythe took a few steps too close to Pap; Pap took a step back. Then Mr. Forsythe turned again to Clem. "You're a miner. You don't waste company time looking for pretties down there, boy." Then he looked at Pap. "You allow this sort of nonsense on company time, Harding?"

Pap rubbed his face and sighed heavily. Then, standing squarely, Pap swung his hammer high and brought it down. He smashed the crystal to bits. A shard of fluorite flashed in the air and hit Clem's cheek. Then, a moment of dead quiet.

Pap straightened his back, wincing with the effort, and

met Clem's eyes. He held the sledge in his two hands across his thighs, slightly swaying. "You muck ore and that's all you do. You don't wander around dreamy, you don't wish away the day. You work, so when it's time to go to grass, you earned the ride up top. Got that, son?" Son. Not an endearment, not even the truth, but a threat.

Mr. Forsythe nodded and walked away. Clem stared at Pap, open-mouthed, but then he snapped his teeth together, bit the inside of his cheek hard enough to taste blood. Everyone was watching him.

Pap's face was red and sweaty, despite the November chill. He jutted his stubble-shadowed chin at Clem, then turned and made his slow way toward the cage. The image of the gentle farmer Tom Gibson filled Clem's mind. His own real father would never have been so cruel.

"You okay, there, Clemmy?" Otto's face was written over with concern and embarrassment.

Clem didn't dare speak, for fear of what his voice might do. The only thing of beauty he'd seen in five long months on the job—smashed to bits. The shattered crystal told Clem what he'd never understood: Pap wasn't ever going to let him quit the mines.

10

THE BELL TREE

"PAP, I DON'T feel good. I'm sick. I've got a stomach-ache. I'm going to have to quit early." Clem practiced his lie in his head, and by midmorning he'd almost convinced himself he really was ill. He stuck his hand into his pocket and felt the rough edges of the crystal pieces he'd groveled in the dirt to save. He was so nervous it was not hard to work up a cold sweat. At nine fifteen, he clutched his gut and moaned. After that it was easy. He rang for the elevator and went up blinking in the light, reported sick to the shift boss, stopped off at the clean-and-change house, and walked away.

At first he lurched along, head down, shoulders slumped, in case the shift boss was watching. As soon as he rounded the base of the giant chat dump, out of sight of the mine and the mill, he straightened his back and quickened his pace. He planned on meeting Lindy at the Bell Tree and working awhile, then getting home before Pap got off shift, and taking a lie-down to keep up the sick act. They'd not notice the missing hours, he was sure.

He did not head immediately for the woods. Instead, he walked briskly through town, up the hill toward home. The truth was, he was scared to work the Bell Tree. What if some drunk started causing trouble? What if someone tried to steal the money Lindy said there'd be so much of? He'd feel a whole lot better with Pally-boy by his side. The problem was sneaking up to the house without being seen and fetching Pal from his spot out front off the corner of the porch. If he got caught, he'd pretend to be sick, like he'd told the boss. If he got to the Bell Tree and Lindy wasn't there, why, he'd just go back to the American B, say he was feeling better, and finish out another miserable day. And if he got to the Bell Tree and Moonshine Man was there, he'd run like hell.

Now he neared the top of the hill, and he dropped into a crouch by the lilac bush. There he hid his dinner pail and dirty clothes. All was quiet. Lightly he ran toward the house at an angle, to avoid being seen from the kitchen. Pally, surprised, stood from his post under the bedroom where Esther, home sick from school, was probably resting, and barked once, a sharp greeting. Clem shushed him, and Pally whisper-barked his understanding. Clem neatly undid the chain attached to Pally's leather collar, and, heart pounding, ran the exposed distance back to the road and over the lip of the hill.

Once it was over, Clem felt better. If he got caught skipping out on shift, they'd be so ashamed of him. Pap never missed a shift. But he wasn't like Pap.

He straightened his shoulders. So what if he cut out on work. He would come home with a pocketful of money, and what was the difference? As long as he brought money home, he wasn't hurting anybody.

Pally-boy barked, and his tongue lolled out of his mouth in excitement. Clem started to run when they got to the woods. Trees crisscrossed the weak sunlight. Clem shivered, approaching the big pin oak where he'd left Lindy that time. The Bell Tree.

"Here's how it works." Lindy held up a small brass bell, with a delicate cherry wood handle, and gave it a little shake. The sound was surprisingly cheerful and sweet, considering, Clem thought. He thought of the thumping of the still that night away over on Mine Lick Creek, unnatural, not right. The little bell, too, was out of place here. She passed it to him.

"Give it a ring."

Jingalingalinga!

The sound made him feel uneasy in his stomach.

"They come, men mostly, once in a while a lady, and they reach up here." She raised her arm over her head, and Clem saw a small shelf settled onto a level branch about six feet from the ground. "They ring the bell, and then they take a little stroll. When they come back, they find a jelly glass of moonshine, and they snort it down and leave the money on the shelf. That's it."

"What if they don't leave the money?" Clem reached for Pally, and Pally leaned against his leg. Clem was glad he'd gone home for him.

Lindy shrugged. "They don't know who's back of the tree," she said. "Might could be my daddy and his friend Mr. Remington." She sighted down the barrel of an imaginary rifle and cocked the gun with a click of her tongue. She dropped her hands and shrugged again. Pally nuzzled her hand. He closed his eyes and whined with pleasure when she scratched his ears. "Might could be this fear-ocious dog back there, for all they know," she said. Pally blinked and gave her one of his gummy smiles.

They took up position in the thicket behind the tree. It was like a tiny room. Walls of twisted vine, roof of arching branches. Three jugs huddled together in the bed of a small, low wagon, which Lindy must have dragged along with her. There was one old metal folding chair, and they both eyed it. Clem swept his hand before him and bowed slightly to mean *Ladies first*.

"Darn right," Lindy said. She unfolded the chair and sat, arms crossed over her chest. Clem sat on the ground, next to Pally-boy, who curled up and began almost instantly to snore.

Clem felt jumpy. He strained to listen for the ring of the bell, keeping a catalog of sounds in his head: Pally's snorts. Light wind in the trees, dead leaves rustling. Birds. Squirrels scampering and tumbling, their tiny feet scratching against tree bark.

"It's quiet," Clem said.

Lindy looked at him. "You don't have to be afeared," she said.

"I'm not."

She lifted one eyebrow.

Clem swallowed. He shouldn't be here, out in the woods, sitting on the cold ground, waiting on who knows who to come way out here for a drink of fire. He should be at work, earning honest money. Pap would kill him. Clem's hands shook just thinking about it. And Ma, her mouth'd drop open and her tongue would tisk and she'd cross her arms and look away, she wouldn't be able to stand to look at him, and Ettie'd—

Jingalingalinga!

Clem jumped. Pally's head shot up from where it'd been resting on crossed paws. Lindy put a finger to her lips. Her gaze cut sharply to the side, listening. Sounds of footsteps rustling away from the tree. Lindy stood, then bent to uncork the first jug in the wagon bed. She filled the jelly jar and held it out to Clem, eyebrows raised, head tipped slightly to one side. An invitation. Clem took the glass from her hand and followed her out the small opening that was the door of their thicket-room, first silently commanding Pally-boy to stay. Lindy looked all around, then jerked her head at him and looked up at the shelf in the tree. Clem reached up and set the glass on the shelf. Then they slipped behind the wide trunk of a black oak some ten feet from the Bell Tree, and knelt there, watching. About two minutes passed, and a man came walking up to the tree. He glanced around furtively, then darted his hand to the shelf, put the glass to his lips, and knocked the moonshine back. He winced, wiped his mouth on his sleeve, and replaced the glass. Looking left and right, he shoved his hand into his pocket and pulled out some coins. He set the money on the shelf, looked all around, and then walked quickly away.

Lindy looked at Clem and winked. "Go on, get it," she whispered.

Clem ran on his toes to the tree, collected the coins, and slipped back into the thicket. All three leaned their heads together over Clem's closed fist. He opened his hand. Two shining coins glinted in his palm. He looked at Lindy and grinned. She snatched one of the coins quick as a magpie.

"Even-steven," she said.

The bell rang regularly, and Clem began to feel more easy. The thicket, although confining, felt almost cozy. Nothing like the dark, underground, buried-alive feeling of the mines. Best of all, his pocket was full of money. He put his hand into his pocket, again, and let the coins move around his fingers.

Lindy had a lot of names for the stuff they were selling: squirrel whiskey. Stagger soup. Tonsil varnish. 'Shine. Sweet spirit of cats-a-fighting.

Clem thought the names rolled out of her mouth as pretty as a poem.

They heard another customer walking up to the tree. Clem peered out to watch this time, feeling a bit more bold.

"It's Bernell Holdman!" Clem whispered to Lindy as she snuck out to set the jelly glass on the shelf. Clem pictured Mr. Holdman stubbing out a cigarette down in the mine and sipping from his Thermos bottle. Clem's hand went to his mouth as if to stifle a cry. He'd never before considered how his own father got the moonshine whiskey in his Thermos that day Clem caught him at it. Clem dropped back away from the peephole, suddenly afraid the next customer might be Pap.

"That fella was definitely trousered," Lindy said, returning to the thicket.

"Trousered?"

Lindy nodded sagely. "Leathered," she said. "Jugged, tangle-footed. Trucked. Tub-thumped."

"Wiggity-whacked," Clem said.

"Say it five times fast, I bet you can't."

"What'll you bet?"

"Your half the take."

Clem smiled slowly, forgetting about Pap, and shook his head. "No sir," he said.

"Try it anyhow, gentleman's bet," Lindy said. "Say tub-thumped, five times fast."

Clem tried and couldn't do it. Lindy doubled over, laughing. Her scarred cheek remained strangely frozen when she laughed. But she didn't seem to care if her black hair swung away.

"You sound like you been hitting the tonsil varnish yourself!" she said.

When Grampy's old wristwatch said one o'clock, Clem got up and stretched. "Come on, Pally-boy, shift's over," he said cheerfully. He thanked Lindy and gave her two good-sized chunks of the fluorite crystal he'd saved for her.

"They're bright as birthday candles!" she said.

As he walked away from the Bell Tree, the sun hung high in the sky, casting from Pal a deep shadow. An ominous feeling pooled in Clem's gut.

He pushed his hands deep in his pockets, pushed down his guilty feeling. After all, what did he have to worry about? Money sifted through his fingers, reminding him of the time he found that heart-shaped rock and brought it home in his pocket for Ettie. Everything would be fine. For now, he thought, maybe he'd be able to work the Bell Tree on his day off, or a few nights a week, if it was okay with Lindy. And Lindy—well, he'd made a friend. He repeated "tub-thumped" five times under his breath, tripping up again, and he kicked a stone ahead of him, feeling happy and full of plans.

Clem picked up his dinner pail and clothes from where he'd stashed them beneath the lilac, and he was already in the door before he realized something was wrong. They were sitting at the kitchen table, in silence. Pap was home from the mine, early. Ma wasn't cooking or washing; she was just sitting there, limp as her apron on the chimney peg. Grampy turned his face—so pale—to Clem, and shook his head almost imperceptibly.

They knew.

Clem looked quickly from Pap's face to Ma's, to Grampy's. He was in an awful lot of trouble, that much was clear. His mouth went dry.

Suddenly Ma dropped her head into her hands and cried out, "Lord! O Lord!" Pap put one arm around her shoulders and wailed, as if in pain.

Clem felt sick. "I'm sorry—it was only this one time, I—"

"Ettie's gone, boy," Grampy said. His loud voice cracked.

"She's in a fit?" Clem started to the back of the house. Why were they just sitting there?

There was a silence. Gone, as in she's run away, then?

It didn't make any sense. He, Clem, had been gone. He'd been gone, out in the woods, gone from where he should have been. Ettie, gone?

Ma cried softly. Pap cleared his throat. "Esther passed in her sleep."

Clem stared at Pap. Tilted his head. "I don't—"

"She's passed, Clem. Your sister's dead."

Clem's knees went loose, and he reached for a chair back. It rocked, righted. He clung to the wood rail as if for dear life, knuckles blanched.

"She'd been down for a nap. Mother went in, and she was gone." Pap put his lips to Ma's bent head, and she raised her chin and looked at Clem.

"I didn't hear anything. Nothing to tell me something was wrong." She looked around the table, then spoke to Clem again. "Where were you?" Confusion creased her brow. She looked at Pap. "You said he came home sick." Her fingers scrabbled the front of her dress, as if she were digging. She pointed one finger at Clem, then curled it back into her fist at her chest.

"I—," Clem began, "I went to the woods—"

Pap raised a hand heavily, waved it off, Clem's words, his explanation. It didn't matter. There could be no confessing.

"Can I see her?"

Pap shook his head. Ma cupped her mouth and stared at him with flat eyes.

"Doc Walton came and got her," Pap said. "She's gone."

Days later, Clem sat on his bed, alone in his and Esther's room. He looked at the blanket behind which her bed was empty, would always be empty. She was gone. He could hardly bear it; she was gone, and it was his fault. What if Pally'd been here? He threw his arms around Pal's neck, breathed his animal smell. What if Pally'd been in his spot outside below the bedroom window? Pally would have sensed Esther's fit, as he'd done before. He would have barked an alarm. Clem pictured himself sneaking up to the house to steal the dog away, to leave Esther unprotected.

Long into the night, Clem tried to make it all go away, but he couldn't. He buried his face in Pally's neck to muffle the endless words, like a bell ringing: Ettie is dead, Ettie is dead, she's dead, she's dead.

Say it five times fast. Ettie is dead. Say it. Say it. Ettie is dead.

11

THE CARDINAL

CLEM HADN'T WANTED to help bear the small pine box. He didn't deserve to carry her slight weight, when he'd failed her so completely. Four men from the mine bore the coffin on their shoulders, and Clem sat with his broken family in the front pew, playing at being the good son. Nobody seemed to suspect the real reason he wasn't a pallbearer was that he couldn't be trusted to hold up his side.

In the weeks after the funeral, Clem often visited her in secret. Now he sat on the packed ground of her grave, his knees drawn up under his chin. A cloud passed over the bald sun of early winter, and sent a shiver through the arc of his backbone.

He dug a small hole in the dirt of her grave; it would be months yet till grass could begin to grow. He'd smoothed a bit of white chert into the shape of a heart, working it with his fingers, pressing and sliding his thumb over the contour of the soft rock; he knew she'd have added it to her treasure chest. Pally-boy watched as he dropped it into the hole and patted it over with dirt, as if planting a seed.

Purdy, purdy, purdy! He turned; something caught his eye, a flash of red. A cardinal. Oh, Esther! Esther, telling him he ought to make a wish and throw a stone.

Without taking his eyes from the red bird, he felt around in the cold dirt until his fingers found a stone. He raised his arm beside his ear and threw the stone at the cardinal. He threw it hard, and a cry came out of his gut and followed the stone across the sky. Then he covered his face with his hands. He couldn't bear to see whether the cardinal flew up or down.

"Clem." He jerked his head up. It was Lindy. He hadn't seen her since the Bell Tree. He hadn't wanted to be reminded of his lying and his shame. She felt uncomfortable, too, he could tell: her hand went to her hair and smoothed it over her scar. Pally-boy put his nose in her hand and waggled all over.

Lindy came close and stood by him. She dug the toe of her boot around in a circle, first one way, then the other way. Her gaze skipped around the stone markers, the barren trees, and the pale gravel road that crossed the three long lines of plots. Old, dry leaves rattled softly on the branches of a cottonwood. She whistled tunelessly.

"It's bad luck," Clem said. "To whistle."

"Since when?"

"Down the mines."

Lindy shrugged. "There's something kind of nice about a cemetery," she said after a while. "It's a sad place, but also don't you feel glad to be alive, when you're here? Like running or shouting?" She looked at him. He frowned. "Oh, not in the way of lucky me, they died and I didn't. I guess I just mean when you know about dying, you know something different about living." She bounced her heel in the dirt and shoved her hands into the pockets of her coat. "Everybody dies. Not everybody lives. I guess."

Clem scratched his elbow. It sounded wise, what she said, but he wasn't sure what it meant. He studied her face. He was half angry with Lindy for trying to offer friendship he didn't deserve. She tipped her head to one side and looked back at him. Pally snorted as if something struck him funny. Suddenly Clem needed to get away from the shadow cast by Ettie's gravestone. He needed to run, just like Lindy said. He stood.

"Come on!" he said, and took off. Lindy chased him till he stopped, breathing hard. Lindy saw a coiled hank of braided rope blown over from somewhere else, and she picked it up and untangled it; they took turns playing with it. First it was a lasso, then a whip. A snake, a skipping rope.

"Don't you know not to skip rope in a graveyard?" came a shrill call. Clem saw Ma coming through the arched iron gate, her face hardly visible behind a big bunch of evergreen foliage she carried. "You'll sever all your strings to God!" she shouted, but she left them alone and walked away from them. Her back was bent and she seemed old. She took small steps, as if careful to avoid stones in the way.

Last week Clem had gone to Miller's and picked out a pretty flower-stitched handkerchief like the one Lindy kept of her mother's. He'd figured flowered hankies must be the sort of thing mothers like. He used money from the Bell Tree. His mother took it and thanked him for the present, but she didn't meet his eyes. He stood and waited. She put the hankie into her apron pocket and turned away, brushing a lock of hair from her cheek, and he recognized that he'd been waiting for her to touch him, to hold him, to rock him like a child.

She never used the hankie, so far as he knew.

Clem started to tell Lindy the woman who yelled at them was his ma, but she spoke first.

"I guess I don't know where in the Bible it says anything about thou shalt not skip rope in a cemetery, do you? What a loony bird."

Clem snorted. "Yeah," he said.

Lindy's gaze followed the lady walking, carrying the jar to the back corner of the cemetery, under the branches of the cottonwood. Watched her stop at Esther's plot, watched her walk right onto the graves there and set the jar on the ground. Even from this bit of distance, the shiny green stood out bright against Esther's gray stone marker.

Lindy's hands flew to her face and she squeezed her eyes shut. "I'm sorry, Clem, I didn't know she was your... I mean..."

Clem snorted again and Lindy opened her eyes.

"Oh, you!" she said. "You snort just like Pally-boy!" Lindy planted her hands on his chest and gave him a shove. Relief flooded him, drowning the painful thoughts about his mother. His heart pounded large and full behind his ribs; he felt he'd burst.

They sat on the rails of the cemetery fence awhile and watched his mother kneeling at Esther's grave, away down the gravel road. Lindy wiggled the rope along the ground from her perch on the iron crossbar. She shook the rope up and down now, rolling it in waves, and Clem caught the end of it.

They heard the crunch of gravel—shh-shh. It was Ma. Lindy hopped down off the rail, flushed with embarrassment.

"Clemson J, you ought to do some tending to things if you're going to be over here anyway," she said, looking at Lindy. Her gaze hung on Lindy's cheek.

"Ma, this is Linda Jean." He waited, but his mother didn't speak. She squinted with suspicion, or judgment. Clem knew Ma had superstitious notions about people who bore scars, that they must have done something to deserve such a sign.

"From school."

Ma stared at Lindy over the tops of her eyeglasses, then took them off and polished them on the placket of her dress. She glanced at Clem, and back to Lindy. Maybe with thoughts of Ettie's white, smooth face.

You're marked. Clem could almost hear her say it, but whatever she was thinking, she kept quiet.

Lindy drew her hair down over her cheek, breaking Ma's inspection.

"Well," Ma said. "We'll see you, then." She put on her eyeglasses, turned, and walked away.

Lindy watched after her, and let out a deep breath. "Must be hard to lose your one and only daughter," she said, still watching the figure walking away, growing smaller.

"Like your mama," Clem said.

"Not a bit like it." Lindy flicked the braided rope in the gravel, stirring the small, pointed stones. "Your ma didn't choose this. It was an accident. She wasn't the one who went away."

Lindy went quiet a minute, then began her tuneless whistling. She stopped, smiled. "You know why I whistle, Clem? Bad luck or not?"

Clem shook his head. "Nope."

"I whistle, and pretty soon some man or lady will say to me, 'Well, you're in a chipper mood today, girl.' I fool them. I fool them into thinking I'm happy and I'm brave. Sometimes I even fool myself." She kicked a pebble up ahead.

"Makes sense." Clem kicked the pebble back.

Lindy looked at Clem. "If I had to work the mines, like you? Down the deep dark?" She pursed her lips and blew a note, high and carrying. "I'd whistle," she said. "Boy, I'd whistle all day long."

12

LOSERS, WEEPERS

THEY WALKED A long way. Their shadows went from falling behind to running ahead as they walked up and down the hilly road toward Abbot Branch. Now they'd arrived at the bank above the moving water. Below them, along the river bottom, stood two small fishing shacks. One was half caved in, and the other had no door.

They sat at the side of the road and watched the cabins a long while, until it seemed certain nobody was inside either of them. Then Clem got up and went down an animal path—deer, maybe muskrat—that wove through the azaleas and the sumac. Lindy followed. He wore a canvas coat but she had on only a woolen sweater that kept catching on twigs. They reached the bottom of the wooded bank and walked on rocks over to the shacks. They picked the nicer of the cabins and went in.

First they set to cleaning it. They brought water from the river, finding a deep eddy from which they could fill the rusted bucket they found in the shack. They washed the grit and dirt from the square of plank floor, and the dust and webs from the single windowpane. Lindy swept the floor with a branch of white pine. Clem took off his canvas coat and used it to beat down the walls, which made Pally-boy leap and prance.

Lindy picked up the dirty coat and snapped it a few times outside the doorway, and then she brought it back in and placed it in one corner, on the clean-swept floor. She went out again and gathered some river rocks and a few azalea sticks patterned with leaves. These she arranged on the coat.

"This is our quilt," she said.

Then she put the rusting bucket alongside the opposite wall. "Here's our pot of stew, on the cookstove."

Clem took out a pack of saltine crackers from his pack, and they sat on the floor beside the window, looking out. An owl sounded from somewhere on the bank, and Clem took his flashlight out of his pack and switched it on, like an evening lamp. It wasn't yet night, but the sun went behind the bank and threw the river bottom into shadow.

Lindy picked at a fingernail. "You got a heart's desire, Clemmy?" she asked.

Clem looked at her across the small pale glow of the flashlight and he frowned a little.

"Sure," he said. "I guess everybody does."

"Well, what is it?"

"It's stupid," he said, and he shivered; he was getting cold. The work of cleaning the shack had made Clem forget everything else for a while, and now he was back in real life; the quilt in the corner was only his old canvas coat. "I want to get out of the mines, is what I want."

"That's not stupid."

"I think it's stupid to want a thing you can't ever get."

Their eyes met over the flashlight, and he shrugged. "You got one?"

She nodded. "To be found," she said. "For somebody to come and find me."

"Your mama, you mean?"

"I guess. I guess that's what I want. For her to come and find me, and keep me." She smiled and lifted one shoulder. "Finders, keepers, right?"

"Losers, weepers," Clem said. He wrapped his arms around his knees and looked out the window, and he saw her eyes in the reflection. "If your mama knew you, she'd be sorry for what she gave up the day she left." He glanced at her. "To go and paint scenery pictures."

Lindy looked down at her boots, and tapped the toes together. Pally dropped his head into her lap. She spoke softly. "Thanks for saying so."

Walking back toward home along the hard road, Clem saw him before Lindy did, and what he saw first was the lion-tamer mustache.

"Quick! It's your daddy!"

They took off running, Pally-boy leading the way.

"Probably heading for the Bell Tree," Lindy said, when they'd slowed to catch their breath. "I'm supposed to be there right now," she said. "My daddy's going to be none too pleased, I can tell you."

"Shouldn't you better go, then?"

She shook her head and pinched her lips. "I'm not going. I don't want to," she said. Her voice shook. "Hey, you want to run again?" Lindy took a few running steps. "I want to run."

"I'll race you!"

They were near town, and so they ran all the way up the hill to the school yard before Clem stopped.

"I won," Clem said, out of breath, and he dropped to the ground and put his forehead to his knees.

Lindy sat beside him and was quiet while their breathing slowed. Clem sat cross-legged, and busied his hands plucking blades of grass.

"I hope you don't get in trouble."

"I'm sick of it," she said abruptly. Pally's ears went forward, on alert, and she ran her hand over his head. "I hate working the Bell Tree. I hate the men, and wondering if one of them's going to want something besides a cupful. And he don't even care about me. I shouldn't have to be there all by myself. I shouldn't have to. I shouldn't have this face!"

She rubbed her face with her palms and sniffed hard. Clem wanted to ask her about the scar, but he hadn't dared to, ever since she'd told him it was a dog bite.

Now he picked another blade of grass. "I had thoughts of it being a way out, for me, that time at the still. Getting into the moonshine business. Isn't that crazy?" He looked at Lindy and shook his head as if asking her, *Was it? Was it crazy?* She nodded, and he went on.

"And then after Pally and I got out of there, even scared, with your daddy shooting at us and everything, even then I couldn't stop thinking there had to be a way out, and I thought another way out would be if my sister just...died.

If she died, then I wouldn't have to go down the mines anymore. And then the Bell Tree—"

Lindy reached out and she grabbed up Clem's hand and she squeezed it, hard.

Clem squeezed back, and then let go.

"I even asked Pap if I could quit the mines now there weren't Ettie's doctor bills. I asked him if I could go back to school. He hit me, that was my answer. He'd never hit me before."

"You didn't mean it like that. You know you didn't make your sister die, you know that."

Clem nodded. He thought he might cry, because Lindy was so nice. She was smoothing her dark hair down over her cheek, a thing he noticed she did when she was nervous. He was afraid they'd ruined something, holding hands.

"I guess we should get going," he said.

"We can stay another little while."

"Okay. Just a little while, then."

They were quiet. Lindy seemed so sad. Clem hadn't told a story or written one down since Ettie'd died, but now he thought of one for Lindy. He looked all around as if there were someone to overhear, and he drew closer to Lindy.

"Did I ever tell you about the time I met a prospector?"

She shook her head.

"Every day he'd pan for gold in the river, just like back there at Abbot Branch. He left everything he had behind— he'd lived over in Annapolis," he added, gesturing north. "Left his wife and child and headed for California to make his fortune."

"Did he find gold? Did he get rich?"

"I don't know," Clem said. "Maybe he did. Maybe he got eaten by a grizzly, or murdered by another prospector. Nobody ever saw him again."

Lindy's eyes narrowed. "He never came back for his wife and child? What a rat."

"Maybe he was a rat, and maybe he wasn't." Clem leaned forward. "All I know is, one morning his boy got up out of bed and went out the house to draw some water. And what do you think he found on the porch step?"

"What? What'd he find?"

"A small leather pouch, cinched tight with a bright blue cord."

"What was in it?"

"Well, the boy opened the pouch and shook it out into his hand."

"Gold! It was gold, wasn't it."

Clem shook his head. "Fool's gold. Oh, it shined, and sparkled, and looked like gold at first. But it wasn't real."

Lindy slumped.

"But you know, the boy didn't care it wasn't real gold. It was as good as gold to him."

"What do you mean?"

"I mean," he said, "when he picked up the pouch that morning, beside it on the wood step was a footprint—wet from the dewy grass. The boy looked around"—Clem looked around—"he called out—nobody answered. But he knew his father had been there. He had come back, if only for a little minute, to give his boy the pouch—holding what he must've believed was a fortune. So it was as good as real gold to the boy."

Clem hugged his shins and dropped his head to his

knees. Pap seemed to hate him now. After all, Ettie was his own child; Clem wasn't. Clem glanced at Lindy, sitting quiet beside him. She looked as though she might cry. Her hand went to her black hair, and she smoothed it absently down over her scarred cheek.

"I guess I'd of treasured a little bag of rocks, too," she said. "Just to know my mama'd had one single thought of me."

13

AN ACCIDENT

CLEM BARELY HEARD the noise, and he didn't recognize it—the sound of slab separating from roof—until the rock fell. A whoosh of air rippled his shirttail, the rock came down that close. He jumped away, thighs burning with the thrill of a near miss.

Clem and Pap and Elmer Schuler were working the area known to the crew as the Ballroom. The tunnel here was unusually high, going up about thirty feet, and broad. Clem was mucking ore and daydreaming about Christmas. He'd been imagining their small fir tree decorated with chains of paper money and strings of real pearls, and beneath it a stash of extravagant gifts worthy of Captain Hook—enough riches to get out of this dark place and never come back.

"You all right, there?" Pap said, his voice unusually high and anxious. He'd been working some feet away, but suddenly he was there beside him.

Pap put one hand on each of Clem's cheeks and squinted into his eyes, and then he let go, took a step back, and looked him over. "You seem all right."

"Yup," Clem said. His head ached and he knew he'd been lucky. He caught himself wondering if he'd mumbled the customary *Glükauf* when he'd stepped out of the cage earlier. Superstitions. Ma would fit right in down here, he thought.

Elmer Schuler shone some light up overhead.

"Looks like the roofmen didn't get everything down before we come on shift," he said, scanning the roof for trouble. "Clem," he said to Pap, "let's us get up there'n take down that loose back."

Clem helped Pap fetch over the ladder from back near the shaft station, and they set it up tall. Clem watched Mr. Schuler climb the rungs up to the top, maybe thirty feet. Pap climbed up behind him, about two-thirds of the way.

"Stand clear, Clemson," Pap called down. Clem stepped close to the side of the tunnel and watched while they reached and scraped at the roof and sides. He heard the sound of scree rumbling down, a pelting storm, and then heavy thuds as several bigger chunks of rock fell to the tunnel floor and lay there.

"Looks to be all of it." Mr. Schuler's voice came from way up. Then several things happened all at once. There was a sharp snap. And then a scream. Mr. Schuler came hurtling down headfirst through the beam of Clem's cap lamp, thirty feet to the floor.

Clem darted his head here, there, till he caught Pap in the light. Pap hung high up, midair in the center of the Ballroom, holding fast to the ladder's safety rope and swinging slowly.

"Pap!" Clem ran and reached his arms to him from where he stood twenty feet below, as if he might catch him.

"Ladder broke! Stand clear!" Pap shouted. Pap slid down the rope as far as it went. He was still ten feet up, dangling and swinging back and forth above the unmoving body of Elmer Schuler.

"Stand away clear!" he hollered again. Clem pressed his back up against a pillar. He shut his eyes tight and put his hands over his face. Pap let himself fall the rest of the way; Clem heard his body thump to the ground. He opened his eyes, saw Pap lying there, and ran to him.

"Pap! Pap! You okay?" Clem's voice broke in a sob.

Pap pulled himself to his hands and knees, nodding and gasping. "Schuler?" he called, his voice tight. His head hung between his shoulders and he was breathing hard, recovering from the fall. There came no answer. "Go see to Shuler," he croaked.

Clem didn't want to leave Pap. His breathing was so ragged. But now Clem was even more afraid of what he'd see on the other side of the tunnel, where Mr. Schuler lay silent. Clem put his hand flat on Pap's back and felt his heart beating strong. His own was pounding.

"Go, I said!"

Clem's cap lamp lit the way. First the light struck upon Mr. Schuler's legs, lying still and twisted. Slowly Clem directed his cap lamp so the beam crept up the man's body and then he saw his head, turned impossibly, knocked aside. An image of a duck at the Joplin penny arcade came into Clem's mind and he shook his head to clear it. He opened his mouth to speak or to scream, but all that came out was breath, gasping quick and shallow.

Clem knelt and pressed around Mr. Shuler's chest, but there was no beat of life.

"What is it, boy?" came Pap's pinched voice from the other side.

"He's dead, Pap!"

Pap groaned, "Ah, Schuler," and then he cried out, loud and mournful, like the bellow of a mule deer.

Suddenly there was another cracking sound, and Pap's scream ripped through the dark.

Clem's searching lamplight moved in violent arcs across the tunnel. He saw a huge slab, fallen and broken across Pap's lower body where he'd knelt on the floor of the Ballroom.

Pap cried out, his face twisted up in pain. "Clemson," he hissed. Then nothing more.

Clem's face was ice cold now. His whole body began to shake so violently crouched beside Mr. Schuler that the dead man's arm fell to the side; Clem scuttled across the floor to Pap.

"Pappy, Pap." He knew he was whimpering but he couldn't help it.

Pap's face was contorted into a terrible grimace. Sweat slicked his stubbled cheeks. Clem whipped his gloves from his hands, twisted them into a knot and pressed it against Pap's teeth.

"Bite down hard, Pap, against the pain." Pap clamped the gloves between his teeth. Then Clem shoved one hand under Pap's chest, feeling around till he got hold of what he was searching for. He tugged at the safety whistle till it gave, and fell back.

Clem held Pap's whistle to his mouth and he blew three long blasts, the signal for trouble.

Quicker than he'd thought possible, four men came,

and the light of their lamps and the noise of their cries and voices filled the space where it'd been just Pap and Clem and death a moment before. One of the men pulled Clem back by the shoulder. Clem pressed up against the rough working face of the Ballroom and squeezed his arms tight around himself.

"Broken ladder," he heard one of the men say, soberly, as they tended to Mr. Schuler and Pap. "Snapped Schuler's back. Let's get him up, boys."

"To grass," he heard one of the men say, the cheerful words this time low and full of sorrow.

Clem stood in the dark against the side of the tunnel, gripping his arms, holding himself together. He would not cry. It was Otto and another man who carried them out on a stretcher. First Pap, then the dead man.

Pap's right-side hip bones were crushed, and several bones were badly broken in his legs. Doc Walton believed he'd walk again, but it would take the bones a long time to heal. The slab had been huge: twelve feet long by six feet across, but thin enough to break when it fell across Pap's stooped body. It was just good luck it wasn't worse. Now it was up to Clem to work the mines alone. Pap said it was important he go right back down to show himself he could. Otherwise, the thought of the accident, seeing Mr. Schuler dead and Pap injured, might give him the shakes. And they needed the money. Clem would be the only earner while Pap healed up.

Now Clem poked his head into the bedroom where Pap was lying in the bed with the crazy quilt over his legs. Pally-boy padded in and sat, looking from Clem to Pap, back again. Ma licked her fingertips and reached to smooth a hank of hair on Pap's forehead. He looked like an old little boy. Clem shifted from one foot to the other. "I'm going now."

"Got everything?" Ma said.

Clem rattled his dinner pail. "Yup."

"You be careful," Ma said.

"I will." Clem gave Pap a little salute. "Don't worry about a thing, Pap. I'll do good work today."

"I know it, Clemson." His voice was weak, almost a whisper.

Pally-boy stood and trotted to Clem's side. Clem stroked his bristled head. "You take care of things, Pally," he said, then turned and walked away.

Grampy raised his coffee cup to him as Clem passed through the kitchen.

"*Glückauf*, boy." His voice sounded heavy and clotted. He cleared his throat, then sipped his coffee, looking with watery eyes at Clem over the rim of the cup.

In the quiet, Clem swallowed, mouth dry. "I wish—"

Pap called out from the back, "Get on, now, you don't want to be late."

Clem swallowed again and lifted his jacket from the peg beside the door.

"Shot of courage?" Grampy held out his cup.

Clem hesitated, then stepped over to the table, took the cup, and drank from it.

"I thought it might be moonshine," Clem said, passing the cup.

"Nope," Grampy said. "Coffee. Strong and straight, just how I like it." He took another sip, grimaced, set the cup down, and planted his forearms on the table. "Hear what I'm saying, now, Clemson. You got all the courage you'll ever need to have. I just guess you do." His words, uncharacteristically quiet, pierced Clem's ears like the clear cry of a hawk.

"But I don't, Grampy." Clem fiddled with his jacket buttons, glancing over Grampy's head at Pap's door. "I thought things'd be different. I'd be different."

Grampy was quiet, polishing the rim of his cup. "You know that big bull pine up the hill there, by the school?"

Clem nodded.

"Well, you and that tree got something in common. You were born into this world on the heels of a disaster, my Jasper taking sick and dying. And that tree rode into town here on a tornado. But I'd say both of you done a good job of sticking around and growing up strong."

He pointed a crooked finger at Clem, and winked. "You remember that, now. I know what I'm talking about."

"All right."

Grampy chuckled. "I got something in common with that old bull pine, too. We're both rough around the edges, with plenty of bark. How do you like that? Ha!"

Clem rocked back onto his heels and smiled. "All right," he said again. He picked up his dinner pail and his change of clothes and pulled open the door. "I guess I'll see you later, then."

"Count on it." Grampy raised his cup of coffee to Clem. "Be right here handy."

Clem wound his muffler around the neck of his wool coat and stepped outside. Clouds of breath trailed out behind him as he walked down the hill into town, and his fingers and cheeks felt numb. He held the pail in one hand and stuffed the other hand under his armpit for warmth. After a while he switched hands.

The lights were on in Travers' All-Day Breakfast. As he passed he saw Mickey in there, sitting in his shirtsleeves at a table with his father. Clem could no more imagine being on the other side of that glass, in the warm restaurant, about to eat a hot meal, than he could imagine shooting marbles with President Coolidge. Mickey's face lit up when he saw Clem crossing the patch of light thrown from the restaurant window. He waved his fork. Clem pulled his hand out of his armpit to wave back, then blew warm breath on his fingers. Mickey's was a different world.

He got to the mine early. Old Saw came over where he stood by the headframe, waiting for the cage to take them down.

"So, young Clemson," he said. "Now you seen your first dead body. Changes a person, don't it," he said, not asking.

Clem shrugged and looked away, swallowed hard, thinking of Esther. He hadn't seen her dead body, but he wished he had, to say good-bye. He thought about Old Saw and his awful stories. All of them about dead people. Did Old Saw used to be different? Did his stories used to be different? Clem turned his head and looked at him out of the corner of his eye. He was picking a tooth with a twig, staring up at the headframe. His legs were straight, skinny pickets running down to feet turned outward. His patched and faded clothes, his wizened body, looked dry and thin and dusty. Clem heard him sigh, watched him glance down and toss the twig to the ground. The old man shuffled toward a couple of men standing by the cage. When they noticed him coming they turned and walked away toward the office, leaving him standing there looking around. Old Saw picked up another stick and started picking his teeth again.

When the elevator operator came, Clem picked up his pail and cap and moved with the other men into the cage. The door clanged shut. He thought about what Grampy had said. He didn't feel courage inside. Not a bit of it. The cage began its screeching drop.

"Man of the house now, are you?" said Mr. Pullen. Clem thought he was poking fun, but he looked at him and he smiled in a way that was genuine. "Your daddy resting comfortable, is he?"

Clem worked his lips over his teeth. "Not too comfortable, I guess."

Mr. Pullen shook his head. "I'd like to think my boy would do the same for me," he said. "Step up, I mean." He looked at Clem again, leaning slightly toward him. "You're what, fifteen?"

"Thirteen."

Mr. Pullen grunted and reached up to fire his lamp.

Clem thought of his birthday, more than six months ago, when Pap'd given him his miner's lamp. How proud and sickened he'd been. He remembered, too, when he was a little boy, trying on Grampy's cap. He'd felt so scared till Pap called him his little man. He'd swaggered around, then. Little Man.

Clem felt a tap on his shoulder. Otto had pressed his way beside him in the cage.

"Let's partner up this shift," Otto said.

Clem fired his cap lamp and nodded. He thought of

Pal, at home, waiting for him. Ma, Pap, Grampy—home, waiting for him, for what he would provide. Feeling rose like bile in his throat; he swallowed, tasted bitterness, fear, sadness, pride. And when the cage stopped and the door clanged open, Otto and Clem walked out into the mine together and began to work.

14

CRACKERS

CHRISTMAS CAME AND went, and though it was a holiday without song or merriment, with it fell a rare snow that stuck and seemed to cover all that had come before, so that Clem began to work the mine in a sort of numb fog for which he was grateful. Ma kept house as always, Grampy kept writing letters to the St. James Lead Company, Pap mostly lay hobbled in his bed, half crazy with boredom and pain. Slowly he began to be able to move about the house. Spring was a long time coming, but the bleak winter months at last gave way.

One evening, Clem and Pap were playing checkers on Pap's bed, and Pap jumped one of Clem's pieces.

"Clemson, I want you to know I'm pleased about what you're doing," he said.

Clem shrugged, uneasy. "I'm not throwing the game, if that's where you going with this, Pap," he said.

"I'm talking about the mines, Clemson, and how you've taken to the work. You've really grown into it. Why, look at those shoulders. Those are the muscles of a miner, and a good one. I hear you're doing good work down there, and with me being off my game, here, well, I'm—I'm just awful pleased." Pap squeezed Clem's shoulder. "You've turned into the miner I always knew you'd be."

Clem sat without speaking. Pally-boy came around the bedside to him and pressed against Clem's leg, and Clem rubbed his velvety ears.

Pap cleared his throat. "Proud of you, son."

Clem's head snapped up to look at Pap. "You never call me that. You never call me son."

Pap scratched the whiskers on his jaw. "Well," he said. "There it is, then."

Clem sat very still. Pap was proud of him. He called him son, because he was a miner. But Clem didn't want to be a miner now any more than he had the day he quit school.

Pap made a move on the checkerboard. "King me," he said.

"Boy! Lulu! Dinner!" Grampy stood on the porch and hollered toward the scrub trees beyond where the patchy dead grass of February gave up. Clem and Lindy were exploring.

Clem stood and made a megaphone of his hands. "Her name is Lindy!" he yelled. "Rhymes with *windy*!"

Lindy grabbed Clem's hand and wiggled it till he dropped his arms to his sides. "It's okay," she whispered.

"You don't have to whisper, he can't hear a word you're saying."

"Funny," Lindy said, "but him calling me all the wrong names makes me feel like he knows me, pays me more attention, than any other grown-up person I ever came across," she said. She rocked back and sat on her heels, her toes bent under and her dirt-crusted hands on her hips.

Clem shrugged, digging around some rocks and debris with his foot. "It's not like he doesn't know you by now, all the times you been by." He saw a corner of wood, dropped to his knees, and put his hands around back of a large chunk of limestone.

"Dinner, I said!" Grampy's bellow came again. "Can't you two hear?"

"Just a second!" Clem yelled. There was something behind the limestone boulder. He bent over, on hands and knees now, and looked closer. "It's a hidey-hole," he said. And he pulled from it a wooden box.

Clem felt as if he'd been kicked in the stomach. He brushed his fingers over the grain, clearing the dirt. The key with the pink ribbon was still in the lock.

"It's my sister's—she called it her treasure chest."

Grampy called again. "I got to yell one more time, you two ain't having any!"

"Come on," Clem said, "I'll show you, inside."

Lindy followed Clem in for the noontime meal. Clem set the box on the table beside his plate.

Lindy sat silent and so did Grampy, looking at the box. Ma came into the kitchen from the back room, and then she saw the oak box.

"Where'd you find it?" she said. She hovered her hand over it, and then pulled her hand back as if stung.

Clem put both hands on the box, protectively. He was afraid she'd take it from him. The treasure chest had been a thing Ettie shared with him. He wanted to be the one to open it.

"Give it here," Ma told him.

Clem could feel the grain of the wood beneath his fingertips. Clem watched his mother drop down into her chair. She seemed to grow older as she sat; in one moment she was his bustling mother preparing the meal, in the next tick of the clock she became this old person who needed two separate movements to get into her chair—bend, then drop, like Grampy. He wondered if she had to pretend all day long. To pretend she hadn't lost her daughter, to pretend her husband would fully heal, to pretend she wasn't heartsick. He was glad, for once, that he worked underground so he didn't have to pretend. He could not be seen in the dark.

She moved her head, and her eyes blinked out at him. She looked tired. "Please," she said.

He lowered his chin and slid the box across the table.

Ma glanced at him, turned the tiny key in the lock, and lifted the lid. One by one, she took out Esther's treasures. There was the heart-shaped stone he'd found in Mine Lick Creek, a blue-green feather, a cuckoo's egg.

Suddenly she shoved the box a few inches away and crossed her arms over her apron front. "Bunch of junk," she said.

Clem looked from Lindy to Grampy, back to Ma.

"I just—I always thought Esther kept important things in this box. I thought when I turned the key just now I'd find something like a gift from her. A sign." Ma cupped her mouth, and then lowered her hand and placed it lightly on her collarbone. "I've heard of people with a loved one gone finding something the departed wanted them to have."

Grampy made a sound like a crow call. "Who on earth do you know got a sign from the dead?" Grampy said.

"Myrna Schuler, that's who. He passed on"—she nodded to Clem, out of some respect for his having been there when Mr. Schuler died, Clem guessed—"and at church she was wearing a cameo pin at the collar of her good cotton blouse. I asked her, Myrna? Where'd you get that lovely pin? And she said she'd found it resting on his empty pillow that morning when she got up, about five o'clock. He'd wanted her to have such a thing, but never afforded it."

Clem exchanged looks with Lindy and Grampy.

"Eat your sandwiches," Ma said.

"Well, these here are things Ettie kept as her treasures, Ma, and I'm the one that gave most of it to her. It wasn't any of it junk to her. It's not junk to me." He half stood out of the chair and pulled the oak box to him on the table.

Ma swallowed and wiped her lips. "I just thought I'd be the one to get a sign," she said. "You don't know what it's like to lose a child."

"I lost her, too, Ma!" Clem said. Lindy reached out as if to try and quiet him, but he waved a hand at her. He felt heat in his eyes and in the bridge of his nose, but he wouldn't cry. "I lost her, too," he said again.

There was a small silence, and then Grampy leaned and put a hand on Ma's shoulder and patted it. "So you hoped for a sign and you got a box of rocks. Children keep collections, is all, Mae! When I was a boy, I collected my own spit!"

Ma put her hand to her forehead. Grampy turned to Lindy. "I had a rubber-stop bottle half full before I gave up on it," he said.

Ma hopped her chair so her back was to Grampy a little, her gray-brown hair bobbing, and Clem saw Grampy wink at Lindy.

"It isn't junk," Ma said, leaning toward Clem. "I know it, Clemson J, it's just that I look at that box and I see a whole mess of things I did not know about my girl. What did that rock look like to her..."

"A heart."

Ma tipped her head. "Yes, exactly, and it looks like a plain bit of chert to me. And it's too late to know her now."

"Mae? Mae!" Pap appeared in the doorway, staggered, and caught himself against the wall. The dark yellow contents of a Mason jar sloshed over his hand.

"Oh, Clem, honestly." Ma hurried to him. "Get back to bed, now."

"Can't a man take a leak?"

"Clem. Please." She took the jar from his hand.

Pap grunted and braced his shoulder against the door frame, then turned and hobbled stiff-legged back to their room.

Ma crossed the room and emptied the jar outside. "I'm sorry," she said when she came back in.

Lindy waved her chunk of bread in the air. "Oh, never mind, I seen worse than that in a jar."

"Well," Ma said. "Thank you." She picked up Pap's dinner plate. "He's not himself."

Ma took the plate back to Pap. They heard the bedroom door close, the low, muffled sound of Pap's voice.

Clem absently fiddled with the ribbon and the key.

"More graham crackers, Lulu?" Grampy asked loudly.

She grinned. "Don't mind if I do, Mr. Harding. They're good. I don't get good crispy crackers like these at home."

Grampy grunted in a good-natured way. "It don't seem like you get any kind of food a-tall over there, Lucky, much as you eat here." Grampy chuckled and looked over at Clem. "Why, Clem here's always restocking the crackers, you love 'em so. Them being your favorite."

Lindy blushed. "Sure makes me feel at home."

"You're welcome," Clem mumbled. He stood and went to the window and looked over the top of the café curtain.

"You're always welcome over here," Grampy agreed, and he reached along the table and patted her hand. "Now have another cracker. I just guess you better had."

"Grampy, the flag's up," Clem said, and started to go to bring in the mail.

"Stay put, boy," Grampy said, using Clem's shoulder to help him up. "Bringing in the mail's about the only time I get up off'n my duff," he said. They watched him shuffle out.

Lindy took another cracker from the waxed wrapping. "I do like it over here," she said. "When I'm old enough," Lindy went on, "I'm going to move somewhere nice."

Clem pulled the curtain aside and looked out. "Where you want to go to?"

"Somewhere with a fireplace, nice and cozy. A cabin maybe. By a river. With quilts, and stew, all my own and no parents at all."

She looked out the window at Grampy, leaning on the mailbox. "I saw a picture plate in a book called *Heidi*. She lived way, way up high in the mountains in her grandfather's house. It was pretty in the snow. Real clean and nice. And that Heidi, she had some sadness in her story, but she was happy anyway, especially in that little tiny cabin." She looked back at Clem. "Maybe someplace like that."

Clem saw Grampy start to make his way back across

the gravel and grass of the yard. He stacked the lunch plates and tableware while he told Lindy about the miners' consumption, and Grampy's weekly letters to the St. James Lead Company.

The screen door banged when Grampy came back in. Clem turned, plates in hand.

"Did the check come today, Grampy?"

Clem heard Lindy take a breath and hold it.

Grampy shook his head. "Nope."

"Confound it," said Lindy, throwing a cracker onto the table. She looked well and truly disappointed. He had that money coming to him, and Clem felt very warmly toward Lindy for believing Grampy'd get that check one day. He felt very warmly toward her for her sense of what's fair, her sense of hope.

Clem hugged the stack of plates to his stomach and thought he felt, in general, very warmly toward Lindy.

"Clem, watch it!" Lindy said.

He righted the plates in his hands, saving the tableware from clattering to the floor.

Later, Clem went to his room; Ma was sitting on the floor, the treasure chest open beside her. He pulled back from the doorway and watched her. With tentative fingers she pulled out the hollow cuckoo's egg, and studied it like a jeweler. She made a gurgling sound deep in her throat, and then brought the fragile shell down hard on the floorboards. Clem heard the sound of the eggshell cracking, soft and final. Then, in a fury, she flailed her hand around inside the box, scattering Ettie's treasures across the floor. Then Ma picked up something from her lap—Ettie's good blue dress. She buried her face in the cloth, and cried.

Clem wanted to cry, too. He'd always secretly thought he was her favorite, because of his real daddy being her first love. Deep inside, she must blame him for Ettie's death, just as he blamed himself. He looked once more at her curved spine, the back of her head, sifting through Ettie's treasure chest. He figured she didn't want to have to look at him. He should be underground, out of her sight. He stepped; she looked up and dropped the dress as if she'd been caught at something shameful, and she turned to Clem, eyes wet and red, searching his face. The way she looked at him, Clem thought, it was just the way she looked at Lindy that day in the cemetery. Accusing. *You're marked.* Clem shifted his feet, and something crunched beneath the sole of his shoe. He looked down, lifted his foot: a bit of shell, pressed flat. He looked quickly at Ma, but she'd turned her attention to Esther's treasures.

He backed across the threshold and left her alone with Ettie.

15

A DRESS

A WEEK LATER, Clem waited for Lindy on the porch, thermos of cocoa in hand. It was his day off, and they'd planned on walking in the woods to the creek, and maybe collecting mussel shells.

He heard her footstep on the porch, heard her voice say his name. He turned, and there she was: it was Esther, smiling, twirling slowly, the folds of woolen cloth, the blue velveteen trim, opening out like a bell around her legs and showing her old brown boots. He shook his head to clear it. It wasn't Ettie. No. The dress looked different on Lindy, with her long dark hair. And Esther'd been shorter than Lindy, but then Ma made all their things with a deep hem to last through growing. It was Esther's good dress, the blue linsey-woolsey. Clem felt cold; he wrapped his arms around his chest.

Lindy picked up her cup of cocoa.

She tipped her head, and when she saw Clem was staring, she smiled prettily. "You like my new dress?" She twirled around again. Her hand went to her cheek. The

motion made him see Ettie once more, giving their old signal, thumb to temple.

Clem's eyes stung. Any second he was going to cry, bad,
like that first day in the mine, when he broke down and all
the men stared at him. Pally-boy pressed against his legs
and whined.

"Please," he choked out. "Go away."

"What—what do you mean?"

"Go!" He turned his head so she wouldn't see the tears
he was fighting back. "Please. Go home. Just go! Please."

"Why—" she began. He could see her reflected in the
window, looking around as if someone else might be able
to explain.

Clem went into the house. He leaned against the door
and gulped back the tears before they could fall. He turned
and peered out the window and saw Lindy standing there
on the porch, steam coming up off her cup of cocoa like
a ghost. She set the mug down on the table, turned, and
walked away.

16

FINDERS, KEEPERS

"HOW'D SHE GET that dress?" Clem asked Ma. Two days had passed, and Clem hadn't seen Lindy at all.

The table was set for supper, and Ma set a bottle of milk beside Clem. "I put Esther's clothes in the church rummage," she said. Her hand stayed on the bottle, as if the glass were holding her up, and she didn't look at Clem. She hardly ever did, now. "We got no use for 'em now."

Clem didn't say anything, but worked his thumbs around the lip of the china cup in his hands.

The third day, Clem said, "I expect Miss Pipe keeps her pretty busy, up at school, if her daddy lets her go." He shoved one arm into his canvas coat, then the other, and then adjusted the collar around his neck.

Grampy took a sip of coffee. "Imagine so."

Clem buttoned his coat. "Well, the shift boss keeps me pretty busy, I can tell you. I don't know how I spared the time to be visiting with her before, anyway."

"Mm-hmm." Grampy's heavy cup made a *thunk* as he set it on the table. He leaned back in his chair, put his hands across his round belly, and looked at Clem. "You haven't got one single notion what it is you're saying, do you, boy."

"Clem! Move it out!" Pap yelled from his bed. "Don't be late!"

Clem grabbed his dinner pail and let the door slam shut behind him.

On the fourth day, Clem came home from his shift and sat with Pally on the porch step. Grampy's old rocker moved rhythmically, and Clem pitched little bits of gravel to the ground in time with the familiar creaks of the chair. Other days and weeks, Clem thought, Lindy would be showing up about now, first her dark head rising over the crest of the hill, followed by the rest of her—the patched and faded dress, the boots, the soft and tuneless whistling. Then he thought of Esther.

"It's just, I miss Ettie more than ever. I miss her." Clem turned his head to glance over his shoulder at Grampy. He'd brought up the mail, and he was fanning himself with the useless papers now that he knew there wasn't a compensation check among them.

Clem turned back again and looked where the patchy grass of the yard met the road, as if he thought she might suddenly rise up there. He pitched another pebble to the ground.

"Also, I miss Lindy."

The rocker stopped squeaking, and Grampy's feet came down on the porch floorboards. "Well," Grampy bellowed, "only one of those two names you mentioned is available. Why don't you just go on over there and call on her?"

Clem twisted on the step to face Grampy. "I can't," he said, "not after I ran her off that way, told her to go home."

Grampy snorted. "Boy, anybody could see that girl ain't one to hold a grudge, not on you." He began to rock again, and he tipped his head in the general direction of Miller Street. "Go on, now. She's a keeper, that Lola."

"I'll think about it," Clem said. He turned around front again. "You want something to eat?"

"Nope," Grampy said. "I ate plenty."

Clem looked up the road. He heard the gentle squeak of the rocker. It was already dark over the hills to the east; the sun was setting pink and yellow over Goggin Mountain. He put his hands on his thighs, and then he stood.

"I'm off, then," he said.

"Good man."

Finders, keepers, finders, keepers, kept stringing through Clem's head as he walked along First Street, left on Main, left again on Miller. All that time, he'd never been to Lindy's. Lindy had always been the one to come over—he figured she wanted it that way.

Clem's palms were clammy. He walked along Miller Street, looking for some detail he could use to match up one of the houses with Lindy, short of knocking on doors till he found the right one.

He saw a man and a woman standing together in a faint pool of light cast by the porch light of a tiny, unpainted house. The lady's back was to him, but he saw right away by her yellow hair it was Miss Pipe. What was his teacher doing there? The man took an unsteady step, sloshing the contents of the tin cup in his hand, and Clem recognized the lion-tamer mustache of Moonshine Man. Lindy's daddy.

He walked up to the house, a sudden cold feeling coating his insides.

"Been gone four days," he heard Moonshine say in a voice slurred with drink. "That girl's a liar and a thief. Stole my tin-can money!"

Moonshine—Mr. Dinsmore—snapped his head to look at Clem, and then Miss Pipe turned. The teacher's face looked pinched and worried, but when she saw Clem she smiled.

"Clemson!" she said, her voice glad. She put her hand out to him, gesturing to come closer.

"Clemson! You're Clemson?" Moonshine clutched at his shirt buttons with one hand, and pointed at him with the other. "She's over this boy's place ever' day of the durn week! What do you know about it?"

Clem didn't even wait one second. He turned around and took off running back down Miller Street. Because in that instant he knew they were talking about Lindy, Lindy who'd taken the tin-can money and run away, and he knew where.

He heard Miss Pipe's voice calling his name. It was dark, and he didn't have a light, and he didn't have Pally-boy. He was afraid of the night, and of Mr. Moonshine, but he was most afraid for Lindy, alone out there. He ran faster.

Clem ran past the mercantile and the church and out along the river road, leaving the chat dump behind him. Twice he jumped into the ditch beside the road and ducked when cars drove by. He wished he'd brought Pally with him; then he'd feel protected. He was alone out here, but so was Lindy. He didn't want anybody to see him, or to lead Mr. Dinsmore to Lindy.

He cut through the pine woods, and crashed through the brushy bank on down to the abandoned shacks on Abbot Branch. It was full dark now, and the moon was up, great and yellow. The sound of his feet on the river rocks sounded dangerously loud. He stopped and looked all around, kneeling while his breathing slowed, and he saw a flicker of light in one of the shacks.

She's there, Clem thought, *I know it.*

He walked with long strides, his feet pressing the river rocks into the sand beneath his boots. At the door, he stopped. He swept his hat off his head, brushed his hair down. He stepped to the window and tapped quietly on the pane with one fingertip. The light went out, but then he saw the dark form of her come across the window. And then her hand pressed against the glass.

She moved from the window, and Clem heard something heavy-sounding drag and scrape away from the door. The door opened, and he slipped inside.

They were both still for a moment, in the near darkness, each looking into the eyes of the other, aware of nothing else; Clem, for one, didn't know how to be friends again.

"Where are the quilts?" he said. "Where's that pot of stew?"

Lindy dropped her stiffness and threw her arms around him. "You found me," she said. "You come and found me."

"Finders, keepers," he said. He released her and his

hands slid down her arms and took her hands. He felt shy all of a sudden, and he looked away.

"I wasn't planning on staying here, you know," Lindy said, looking around as if the ramshackle place was her failure, a reflection on her housekeeping skills. "I figured I could make some money and then I'd go on my way to find her."

"Your ma?"

Lindy nodded. She picked up a little knob of pink and purple fluorite from the crate that was her table, and slipped it into her pocket. Her face reddened.

The door latch rattled and Clem jumped to his feet.

"Linda Jean!" came a man's voice from the other side of the wood planks.

"What do you want to do?" Clem whispered. "What do you want me to do?"

There was a thud, something hitting against the door. Lindy took a deep breath, then she smoothed her hands down over her thighs and opened the door.

Mr. Dinsmore smelled of whiskey and he gripped the neck of a bottle in his hand. A rifle pointed from the crook of the other elbow. He looked at Clem, and from Clem to Lindy, and back to Clem.

"Friend of mine seen you," he said, pointing at Clem. "Hustling out the River Road." Pivoting on his heel to face Lindy, he stumbled, recovered. He raised the bottle to his wet lips without taking his eyes from Lindy, and then tipped back his head to drink. He wiped his mouth on his sleeve, and then dropped his arm, letting the bottle bounce against his hip. He stood swaying between Clem and Lindy.

"C'mon, girl," he said, tipping his head toward Lindy.

"Truck'sh up there. I got the truck. I gotta make a run t'night." His wet lips twisted into a cracked smile and he jiggled the whiskey bottle.

Clem glanced outside, and could see headlights staring blankly through the trees, far up the bank where the road ran.

Clem looked sideways at Lindy, and cleared his throat. "I don't think she's going with you," he said, drawing Moonshine's unfocused gaze.

"Thish th' little man of the house?" Mr. Dinsmore gestured with the bottle at Clem. The whiskey in it made a sloshing sound, strangely high-pitched. "He why you run off?"

"Daddy"—Lindy took a step away from him—"I don't want to do the Bell Tree anymore." Mr. Dinsmore jerked his head to her and took a moment to focus, his head tilting to one shoulder. His jacket was filthy and he smelled like fish. "If it's all right," she said. Her father tipped his head back again to drink from the bottle.

"It is not all right," he said. He shook his head slowly, once to each side, while keeping his eye on her. "It is not all right. You got to do it on account I'm your daddy, and you do as I say." He took another swallow, drew his sleeve across his mouth. "I own you."

Lindy shifted her eyes to Clem, and Moonshine saw and snapped his head in Clem's direction. He was glassy-eyed. Drunk. His arm with the bottle swung in an arc as if to fight for balance, nearly hitting Lindy in the face. She flinched.

"Don't," Clem said. "You'll hurt her."

"What?" The man fell back one step. "Little man going to step in, is he?" Again the bottle swung out, and Lindy ducked. Clem took a step toward Moonshine, and the man took his rifle in one hand and jerked it into position. He stumbled and looked to each side, as if it were difficult to choose between the gun in one hand and the bottle in the other.

Clem reached in and grabbed the barrel of the gun with both hands and pushed it up. The gun hit Moonshine's chin. His head jerked back on his neck and his eyes rolled up, showing the whites. Clem pulled the gun from him and hurled it against the door. Then he grabbed the bottle and he smashed Moonshine over the head with it. The bottle broke above his ear, cutting his scalp. His knees buckling, he stepped forward and righted himself, then he bent at the waist, bleeding from the side of the face onto the clean-swept floor. Clem waited, the broken bottle like a pickax ready at his shoulder.

Lindy looked at the jagged glass of the bottle and the blood pooling on the floor. She sank to her knees and then fell against the wall, covering her head with her arms and crying in a high-pitched keen.

"Lindy, it's all right," Clem said. "It was like my sister in one of her fits," he said. "You went away from me." He stroked the back of her hand.

She was quiet now; whatever demon had consumed her was now burned out.

"He's gone. I turned him out." Clem peered into her eyes, behind the black curtain of hair, damp from tears. He said again, "I turned him out. He passed out, and then when he got up again he must've just been too drunk to fight anymore. He was bleeding, but he kept saying he had to make a run. Truck's gone."

She reached her hand to her hair in the familiar motion, but she pushed it to one side and curled her fingers around the hook of her ear, tying back the curtain from her face. An owl called from somewhere in the woods, and Lindy took a deep breath.

"She's not coming for me," she said.

17

STORIES AND LIES

LINDY TOLD CLEM everything. When she heard the crack of the bottle and saw the jagged glass, and the blood, she remembered.

"He wasn't always a drunk, my daddy, but he drank," Lindy told Clem. "In and out of work, in and out of the house. One night he came in drunk and he hit my mama. She was going to have a baby. Mama screamed at him to get out, and he screamed back, 'You can't turn me out of my own house, my own son about to be born.' Mama yelled at him, 'How do you know it's a son?'"

Lindy looked out the window of the cabin. "Mama wore a brown dress with climbing leaves and bright little flowers." She turned to Clem, and her face clouded again. "'I just know in my gut it's a boy,' daddy said, 'and then things will turn around, with a son.' And Mama, she said something in a low, hard voice, and he got so mad he smashed the bottle in his hand against the table edge."

Lindy's mouth twisted as if she tasted something bad. "All of us just stood there looking at that broken bottle he was gripping in his hand. We looked at it and I saw mama's face—she looked so scared, I'd never seen her that way. I remember she put her hands over her belly and backed away." Lindy shook her head. Her eyes glistened with tears that hadn't fallen. "And then he pushed her down, and she screamed again. And I—I ran and I jumped on him, scratched at his eyes and face, and I was crying and screaming right into the side of his head." A few fat tears spilled over onto her cheeks and she wiped at them. "I bit him. I bit down on his ear, hard as I could. And he swung away with the bottle in his fist, and that was all I knew." Lindy looked at Clem and blinked. "When I woke up, I was at the neighbor's place, a mile away. They said mama left to have the baby somewhere safe."

Now Lindy lowered her head and drew her sleeve across her eyes and cheeks, wiping the tears. "I never seen her since."

Lindy turned to look at Clem. "That's what happened. That's how I got this," she said. She slapped her own cheek. *Slap!* And again. Clem grabbed her arm to stop her.

"It's all a lie," Lindy said. "My daddy did this, and she knew it, and she left without me. She's not coming for me." She rubbed her face with both hands, took in a deep breath through splayed fingers, dropped her hands to her lap.

Clem lit another of the candles and set it on the floor and then sat down on the floor beside her.

"But, Clem," she said, her head hanging, "if I don't pretend she's a different kind of mama than she was, and tell myself my pretend-mama's coming to find me, the good one I made up..." She lifted her head. "I can't hardly understand how my own mind could trick me like that. I half believed it. That she went away to paint pretty pictures, that she'd come find me and take me in, and that we'd be so happy."

Clem nodded. "It's okay," he said. He fiddled with the candle, dipped his fingertip in the hot wax, rubbed the thickened coating with his thumb. He thought about the stories he made up for Esther, Old Saw's horrible true-life tales, Lindy's many lies about her scar and her missing mother.

"I think," Clem said now, searching for the words, "I think sometimes a story is the only way to get through it." He looked at Lindy. She had to be brave every single day. "Something inside you made it up without you really knowing it, to protect you," he said.

"But it wasn't true," she said, shaking her head.

Clem looked up for a long moment and saw the crossbeams above their heads, the failing roof raised over the slender beams, a glimpse of black sky through a hole in the boards. He let out a long breath, then reached his hand to her face. Carefully, his fingertips traced the edges of the damaged place, the single wax-coated fingertip numb like her skin.

Lindy pulled away. "I can't even cry about her now," she said. "I'm all cried out." She rubbed her eyes with her fists and her voice caught. "I don't know what I'm going to do."

They both were quiet for a while.

"You want to hear a story?"

"Not really," she said. "Not right now."

"Not a made-up one. It's just something I guess I never told anybody," Clem said. "It's that I never cried over Esther. I don't know why I can't; it's like I'm not allowed."

"Who? Who won't allow it?"

He shook his head. "I don't know. But when I saw you wearing Ettie's dress I thought I was going to. Thought I was going to crack wide open and spill out all over the ground." His mind saw the smashed crystal sparkling near Pap's boots. "That's why I told you to get away."

Lindy picked at the frayed hem of her cotton dress. "You can get over somebody dying," she said. "Or leaving." She glanced at Clem. "But what you can't get over is feeling like you're the one to blame."

Clem thought of Pap, how he wasn't ever going to let him quit the mine. And Ma. It seemed she hardly ever looked at him anymore since Ettie died. Like she couldn't stand to see him standing there breathing.

An owl called again, close by. A few moments later another call came from the other side of the shack. Lindy leaned back, reached into a pocket on the front of her dress, pulled out a folded cotton handkerchief, and handed it to Clem.

"One of these days you're going to cry," she said. "And when you do, you can use this."

Clem unfolded the cotton square and recognized the flowers and the stitching.

"This is hers."

She nodded. "I was keeping it nice."

"Thank you, Lindy," he said. "I give you my word, I'll

blow my nose all over the darn thing." He leaned to one side to slip it into his back pocket.

She smiled, her cheeks wet.

"We can wait till light to go back," he said.

"No," she said. "I'm cold."

"Okay," he said. "We'll be able to see. It's a big moon."

She reached to redo the lace of one boot. "Now I'm going to have to think what to do. I still got my secret money. Maybe I really will run away one day, far away."

They left the shack and made their way up the bank to the road. "There's plenty of time," he said. "It'll be all right." But he knew it wouldn't be all right. She'd have to go back home. Her daddy would be mad as hell. He'd cut her face with a broken bottle when she was just a little girl; who knew what he might do to her?

"It'll be all right," he said again. He spoke as if it was the truth, and Lindy started to cry a little. She took a step closer to Clem as they walked along the river road, reached for his hand, and he took it.

"Why are you crying?" Clem's voice was soft.

She shrugged. "I'm just a big fraidy-cat, I guess. Too afraid to run for it. I probly got a brother or a sister somewhere I'd like to meet. But I'm too scared to go and see."

Clem squeezed her hand, and Lindy sniffed loudly.

Watching her rub her nose, walking along, he had a funny thought. Turned out he did have one, single thing in common with Pap. He didn't want Lindy's gratitude, just as Pap hadn't wanted Ma's. He wanted her heart. Happily, he kicked a rock in the way, sent it skittering down the road ahead.

"Thanks for getting rid of my daddy back there," she said.

"He'll be back."

"I know it," she said, hugging his arm. "But at least he'll have a pretty stiff headache."

18

MARCH 18

MARCH 18 DAWNED warm. Strange for March. Clem walked down the hill toward the American B. At that gray, early hour, the light was thin, the air was muggy and hung close. Clem passed the Tunnel Tavern and Miller's. The buildings huddled around the base of the giant chat dump like baby pigs around a huge sleeping sow, and a fiery glow cast by the mill around the other side threw the hill into a hellish silhouette, black against red.

Just after the noon dinner break, Clem lifted his shovel as he'd done a thousand times, and it was easier than it used to be. He felt muscled, like Otto, and he smiled. He lifted his shovel once more and let it fall and catch a load of ore, and right then there came a rumbling, and the lights went out. He thought he'd caused it to happen, somehow, with that *thock* of the shovel. He caught Otto in the beam of his lamp, and Otto gave him kind of a shrug and a "Humph." After a minute of scratching their chins and wondering what it was all about, the men all went back to their work.

But only for as long as it took for the bottom boss to reach them from his underground station. He'd been running.

"Big rush of air blasted the door off the ventilation shaft, collapsed some timbers," he said. He bent over with his hands on his thighs, and the men mumbled and waited while he took a few deep breaths. He hauled his head up again and looked around at the faces of the crew. "Maybe an explosion in some part of the mine," he said. "Best get out of here."

The bottom boss was a big-faced man. Clem wondered if he might have a heart attack, that big face was so tight and shiny, his breathing was so hard. "No power to run the cage," he said. "Let's go."

The workers began to pick up their pails and gather the shovels and picks.

"Leave 'em," said the bottom boss. He started up the main shaft, climbing the narrow stairs that ran beside the elevator. The men started following him.

Clem fell into line. They climbed a good half hour before word came down from up top, passed man to man down the line. "Twister." If they were right and it was a twister, what would they come up to when they climbed out of the shaft?

Sawyer, in the dark, began to whisper. "Mortician's wife, down in Tennessee, she opened the front door on a twister, and got sucked right up into the eye of it, up and out the house. They found her dead body in a field. Not a mark on her. Hairdo weren't even messy."

Somebody told Sawyer to shut up, but mostly all the men were quiet, breathing heavy with the work of climbing the steps. The bitter excitement Clem had tasted in his mouth before was shadowed by a colder feeling: fear. He wished Pap were there. Couldn't this line of men go any faster?

"Another time, I heard of a brand new baby yanked right out of his mama's arms and never found at all."

Shut up.

"Worst I heard was when Amos Pike, rest his soul, was a boy. He picked his way home after a twister and found his granny sitting in the middle of a field where the house had stood, sitting in her old rocker." Clem felt a tap on his shoulder and he glanced back. Old Saw made a slice across his throat with his hand. "De-capitated."

Clem trudged on and tried to block out Old Saw's voice. Maybe Ma was hurt right now and Pap not able to go to her, and what if it was Grampy sitting in his rocker without his head. The shaft was so narrow. Would the creaking wooden steps hold, with the heaviness of all the men climbing and climbing? Clem didn't know if he could stand it. The whine of Old Saw's voice behind him went on and on. His breaths came shallow and his eyes stung; he just couldn't do that in front of the men, he wasn't going to cry. He stopped and turned around on the step, put his hands on Sawyer's shoulders, and shoved him as hard as he could. The old man landed full in Otto's chest and the two of them fell back a couple of steps and stopped.

"The hell you doing?" Old Saw's face showed shock and outrage.

Clem turned away and shook out his hands as if they were dripping. Then he wheeled back at Sawyer. "We've all got people up there!"

Sawyer rubbed his shoulder. "I don't."

Clem looked hard at him, and there was such a fiery feeling in his gut he thought he might kick him. Then he glimpsed Otto's face behind Sawyer, grave and worried.

"I'm sorry for you, Sawyer," Clem said, finally. "I'm sorry."

Clem turned and started climbing again, closing the gap between him and the next man. His legs burned. Ten stairs, then turn, ten more stairs, turn again. He counted under his breath, and then he heard singing.

His eye is on the sparrow, and I know he watches me.
Though by the path He leadeth, but one step I may
    see.
His eye is on the sparrow, and I know he watches me.
Whenever I am tempted, whenever clouds arise...

Clem could only whisper the words. But he imagined the voices of the men rising over their heads and out the hole in the ground like bats from a cave. He imagined the men climbing out to meet whatever was up there, finally knowing, while the rest followed slowly behind, still in darkness, climbing toward the surface, step by single step up the narrow shaft.

The feet of the man ahead of him were gone abruptly, and then it was Clem's turn. Hands reached to help, and when his head cleared, the first thing he noticed was the sky, beautiful blue, with puffy white clouds floating calmly. But there had been rain. His boots sank in thick black mud, and his nose filled up with a rotten, dank smell—turned earth and wet wood and smoke.

The men were all running away around the chat dump toward town in a frantic stream, like ants pouring from their ruined hill.

Clem stuck with Otto, pulling through sucking mud up to their knees. They could hear men crying out and yelling, awful sounds, up ahead. They made their way around the chat dump.

"Lord!" Otto cried out. "Lord!"

The town was leveled. No Tunnel Tavern, no Miller's. Nothing else, no other building, was recognizable. It was all in smoking heaps of sticks and debris. There were fires going all over. Clem's heart pounded. Did Ma have the cookstove going when the storm hit? Was their place on fire?

He was alone. He'd been standing with Otto, but Otto had gone, or Clem had gone. He looked all around, gasping, confused, terrified.

"Hot wire! Hot wires all around, Clemson!" A man grabbed Clem's arm and held it hard. "Mind where you step!" he shouted. Clem stared at him. The man knew Clem's name, but Clem didn't know who he was. He pulled back. The man frightened him; his face was black with what looked like whiskers. But it was splinters, Clem saw. The man's face was full black all over with splinters.

He looked where the man pointed, at a sparking wire dancing on the ground. He moved out of the way and the

141

splinter-face man left him. He looked around, trying to get his bearings. There was nothing to distinguish Main Street. There were no landmarks. No trees, no houses, only smoking wood and piles of rubble everywhere, and the fires, and people screaming, all of it all at once. He put his back to the chat dump to get his direction, and dragged his feet and legs through the sucking mud up the hill.

Bushes and trees were stripped of all their budding green. Clem passed by a single power pole standing. A hay-straw was driven straight into it like an arrow.

His face was wet. He heard, as if from far away, mewling noises from his own throat. A barber chair lay across his way—Leadanna had no barbershop. After a while he saw Otto climbing over a pile of broken lumber. Clem reached to grab Otto's hand, but he was too far away.

The smell almost overcame him—dank, like dirt and wet gunmetal and something else he couldn't name. And the smoky dust—his mouth filled up with it, he could feel the grit in his teeth, and he tasted metal, like a coin on his tongue.

Clem looked up, and then he stared, trying to make out what he was seeing. He was looking right into the rooms of a giant dollhouse. Otto came near. He took hold of Clem's arm and pulled him. But Clem stood there unable to move.

"That's the Lever place," Clem said to Otto, scared. He knew because it was one of only a few houses in Leadanna with an upstairs floor. "The front's off it!"

Clem heard Otto speak above the ringing that had begun in his ears. "Come on, Clemmy." Otto's face was ashy white and his eyes were wild. Clem grabbed for Otto's hand and Otto took it up and didn't let go.

Searing pain shot through Clem's foot. He gasped and raised his leg. A board came up with his boot. He set the foot down and put his other foot on the board, then yanked upward to free the foot from the board. A ten-penny nail stuck up out of it. The nail had driven straight into and through the bottom of his boot. He limped on.

When they had worked their way higher up the hill they saw Otto's house. Otto lived in a white house with just his ma. It was only the two of them; his father'd been killed in an automobile accident out on the north-south road. Otto had painted the clapboards himself in the summer. Now the paint was stripped completely off it. The only reason Clem knew it was Otto's place was that his ma was standing out front. Her yellow dress shimmered in the sun.

Otto broke away from Clem, yelling to her, and she turned, reached out her arms, and cried his name. Otto turned to Clem, a big smile across his face. "To grass, Clemmy!" he called out. He waved. "To grass!"

Clem kept going. He looked back and saw Otto stroking his mother's head as if she were a little child. Otto waved to Clem once more, as if everything would be all right. Clem turned toward home again and quickened his pace. The pain in his foot was almost unbearable. The smell of smoke was everywhere.

Finally Clem was limping up the hill—the mud wasn't so thick here. And then he was home, and—thank God!—it was still standing. The roof was clear off it. But otherwise, it looked okay. Clem began to run, stagger-step.

Everything was eerily quiet. No birdsong, no barking, no wind, as if every living thing had learned some information he wasn't yet aware of. He didn't want to call out into the silence. What would he do if there was no answer?

"Ma?" he said. His voice cracked in the air. Ma didn't call back to him; no one did.

Clem walked up onto the porch, cold spreading through his chest. He could hear a wailing. From down the hill in town, sirens keened. His teeth began to chatter. The door was off its hinges, and Clem stepped inside the house. No one was there.

"Where is everybody?" he whispered. "Where are they? Where's Pally?" And Lindy, he thought, his heart racing, and Miss Pipe and Mickey and—and Lindy, he thought again. "Ma! Pap! Where are you? Pap!" he called out, this time loudly, up to the sky, where the roof should have been.

Then suddenly he knew where they must be. The storm cellar. He went back outside, but he couldn't spot the bulkhead door to the cellar in the ground. Confused, he turned all around. The roof had landed on the ground behind the house, and some trees were down. Everything looked different. He listened. Muffled voices, calling. The noises were coming from under the roof, and then he knew that the roof had fallen on the cellar door, locking his family inside.

Quickly Clem began to pull at the roof, but it was too heavy and bulky. He pried off a board, and then used it to lever part of the roofing up and off the cellar door.

"I'm here!" he called. "I'm going to get the roof off the door. I'm going to get you out!"

Clem worked steadily, pulling at the boards and the plywood under-layer of the roof till finally he freed enough of the cellar door that Grampy was able to push it open from below. Suddenly Clem was looking down the short, steep run of stairs into the blinking faces of Ma and Grampy and Pap all in a row, like the glass Ball jars of green beans and succotash lining the cellar shelves.

"Oh, thank heaven, Clemson J," Ma was saying. "We didn't know what was happening at the mine, if you were okay." She winced when she spoke.

"I tripped, getting in here in a hurry, and broke my tooth," she said. She shook her head. "Thank heaven," she said again. "If that was the worst of it for us, then I'm more than glad to bear it."

"Help me get your pap up now," said Grampy.

Clem leaned over the lip of the cramped cellar, and he and Grampy managed to push and pull Pap up out of the ground. They all rested in the yard, breathing heavily.

Clem spoke first. "Where's Pally-boy?"

Ma and Pap looked around, but Grampy groaned and ran a hand across his face.

"I saw that greeny gold sky," Grampy began, looking to the horizon as if he could still see the tornado coming on. "We quick yanked your pap from his bed and between us we hustled him out to the root cellar and lowered him down in. And then I was going to go back up and fetch the dog in here, but—the force! I could barely push the door open, and when I got it cracked, that's all I could do, boy! I could only watch."

Clem shook his head. "Pally-boy!" he called again.

Grampy waved a hand in the air, his bony fingers circling. "I saw him lift off the ground," he said, his voice a hoarse whisper.

"Pally!"

Grampy swallowed hard and grabbed Clem's arm. "Wind took him up, and he hovered there, four feet off the ground." Grampy let go, and Clem rubbed where he'd been holding on. It hurt.

"And I saw him barking but I couldn't hear nothing excepting the roaring. Roaring like a dozen freight trains. And then I saw him shoot straight up into the sky, the chain holding him fast by the neck like some awful kind of kite."

Clem stared at him. He shook his head. *No.*

"It's true," Grampy whispered. "I saw. He was turning about thisaway and thataway, twisting from his neck. He'd had to choke to death."

Clem stood and began to back away. "No," Clem said. "Pally-boy, come here, boy!" He didn't want to hear any more, but Grampy kept talking.

"And then the roof, it lifted off and the cellar door slammed down, and you know the rest. Couple minutes later, the whole place gone quiet as a grave, and we been waiting here, just waiting to know if you made it."

Clem's legs went weak, and he sat back down on the ground. Ma took his hand.

"I'm sorry, Clem," Pap said. "He was a good dog."

Clem was silent. There wasn't anything to say. His heart squeezed in his ribs.

"It's awful sad, Clemson J," Ma said. Her *s* sounds lisped through the gap of the missing tooth and made a whistle, and Clem thought again of Lindy. He prayed that she was somewhere safe, whistling to be brave.

19

AFTER THE STORM

SPLINTERED. BROKEN. SHATTERED, riven, wrecked.
Stories and pictures coming together, bit by horrible bit,
every blink of the eye some new and ghastly shock, the
shards assembling, finally, into a terrible new world. Clem
could take in only pieces at a time. He heard the stories,
told his own. Every story sounded like a lie.

The townspeople cleared rubble by hand. Sheets of tin,
shattered glass, bricks and boards, utility poles, an uncashed
paycheck, a crushed piano, splintered legs of a painted
table, a feather bed, a sow. How the life of a town could be
heaped so, into a useless pile, threw Clem into foggy confusion. Leadanna was a mess of precious belongings, like
the rocks and shells of Ettie's treasure chest—now without
meaning, without a key.

They all came, dozens, by train—the Red Cross from
St. Louis, the Christian Scientists from Boston, doctors
and nurses from St. Genevieve and Bonne Terre, construc-
tion men from as far away as Colorado and California—and
in the space of two days, work began in Leadanna and all

along the path of the tornado, following where it had torn up the Lead Belt and barreled on into Illinois at eighty-five miles per hour all the way to Indiana, hundreds of miles away, where it had simply died out. The papers described the cyclone in far-away weather terms, words about the two great black clouds that seemed to crash together, the wind that roared, the huge rolling mass a mile wide. A category F-5 tornado that went perfectly straight, no skipping or zigzagging, raging wild for three hours steady, like no cyclone ever seen. And when they could finally figure the numbers, the papers counted six hundred ninety-five dead, or missing and thought dead, and two thousand hurt. In Leadanna, they held seven funerals in a Pullman railroad car.

Clem looked again at the newspaper report. He knew every name that was there, but still he needed to feel the words under his fingers; he'd smudged the print. Once again, his heart made a fist when he saw the name of his friend Otto Pickens. Poor Otto had made it all the way home, only to die in a fire that smoldered like a secret in the back of the house and bloomed and roared to life after everything'd gone quiet.

Ma sat across from him at the table and touched the back of his hand. "Good people," she said. Clem nodded. "Good, dear friends." Ma sniffed, and Clem looked at her. "It's so hard to lose them," she said, her head shaking side to side. "So very hard." She gulped. "And you never forget them, Clemson J, you just never do. And that's good. It's good that we knew them, even though it hurts so badly." She pulled a hankie from the ribbed cuff of her sweater and wiped her nose, and Clem noticed it was the one he'd given her after Ettie died, the one he'd bought with the Bell Tree money.

"You had more than your share, I guess," he said, and she nodded and took a quick breath.

"God gives out no more than we can bear," she said. "That's what they say, anyway, and I suppose if I'm still standing, then it's true." She smiled sadly. "And you're still standing, too, Clemson J."

Clem looked down at the table. "That day, when Otto saw his ma, and he ran to her, I didn't even think to go with him to see if everything was all right there. I just went running home."

"Of course you did, lovie. And we needed you to come home." She leaned back and looked at him from another angle. "Do you think you could have changed anything?"

Clem shrugged. "No. I guess not. I guess I didn't whip up any tornado, anyhow." He tried to smile.

Grampy came in and poured himself a cup of coffee, then poured another which he set in front of Ma, and then lowered himself into the chair beside her.

Ma took a sip of coffee, and leaned toward Clem across the table. "Clemson, none of this was in our hands, not a bit of it. Not your daddy dying, not Esther, not your friends or your dog. We love them, and we'd do anything to hold on to them, and we can't. We don't have any say in the matter. We just don't."

She took off her eyeglasses and wiped them absently, and it was quiet while Grampy sipped from his cup.

"We can't go thinking things coulda been different if only we did this, or we didn't do that." Ma put her glasses back on and shook her head fiercely. "You think I didn't blame myself for your daddy getting sick and dying?" she said, her voice rising. "For Esther? Well, I did. I asked myself a thousand times, what if I'd followed that ghost dog? Would your daddy have died? What if I missed a sign, about Ettie?"

Grampy started to cough, and Ma thumped his back as she fixed her gaze on Clem. "I know you think it's foolishness. But when your life seems unknown to you, and things happen so out of the blue, you look for reasons. You look for ghost dogs and you watch for signs the angels are too interested in your babies." She pushed her chair back and tucked her hankie back into her cuff.

"I wish they could list Pally-boy in the news," Clem said. He felt the loss in his gut, like hunger.

"Course you do." Grampy coughed, gripped Clem's shoulder. "It's too much for one lone boy." He shook his head, coughed again, the sound like shoveling gravel. "It's your boyhood's what it is. Blown away on the wind." Grampy took the newspaper and folded it, then got up and put it away in the cupboard.

They left Clem alone at the table, and he sat there awhile, thinking about what Ma had told him. She didn't ever blame him for Esther, and he knew that now.

Clem went and got the newspaper from the cupboard. His finger traced the names once more, and found the one he didn't want to see.

Linda Jean Dinsmore. They'd searched for three days, but never found her body. There was no casket for her funeral.

Clem put his head down on the newspaper; at last, he wept.

20

THE SCHOOL YARD

"HAND ME THAT hammer, would ya?" Orval Pullen interrupted Clem's thoughts. They were working on the new church. Clem picked up the hammer and passed it up to Mr. Pullen where he was straddling a crosspiece.

"It's going up right quick," Mr. Pullen said. "You're doing good work on those bricks, Clemson."

Clem nodded, slapped a pile of mortar on a brick, spread it, set the brick down on the row already in place, picked up another one. Mrs. Pickens had asked Clem to deliver the eulogy for Otto. He'd written out some words, but wasn't set on what to say. He placed another brick. Then again, and again, counting bricks, like Esther counting her treasures. A brick for Otto Pickens. A brick for Pal's sorry game of fetch. A brick for Esther's white-blonde hair. A brick for Lindy's ruined cheek.

"Here's that hammer back," said Mr. Pullen. Clem took it and passed it on to Mickey's father. A splotch of mortar fouled Mr. Olsen's handsome leather shoe. He remembered talking to Mickey on his last day of school, when he thought such a family could never be touched. But everyone had been touched.

Clem stretched his arms above his head, pulling and testing the tender muscles in his shoulders, and he caught sight of the tipple going up. Work would start again at the American B once the area was cleared and the mill repaired, with crews on short shifts so that all available men could both muck ore and help rebuild the town.

He dropped his arms, brushed his dusty lips with his shirt cuff, picked up the trowel.

Later, Clem took his dinner pail up the hill to the ruin of the school, where he might be alone and quiet. He was hungry, but he ate without tasting, sitting amid waste and debris on a piano stool that came from elsewhere. He looked at the demolished building, where he'd spent so many good days in the company of Miss Pipe, and always, over their shoulders, the knob of Goggin Mountain. From here, he could see the path the tornado took, from just south of the mountain, straight through the school building, tearing it down to scraps, sparing the lone bull pine born of another tornado, then barreling roughly down Main and Miller streets, roaring through town. Grampy'd said the sound was like a dozen freight trains; how frightened Ma must have been! And Lindy. What went through her mind in her last moments? He was ashamed to wonder if she'd had a thought of him.

When he'd finished his dinner, he went and rested up against the solid trunk of the big pine, still standing. Grampy had compared him to the tree; he was glad the tornado hadn't beaten it. Sun warmed his outstretched legs. He closed his eyes. An insect buzzed past his ear, and he swatted at it halfheartedly. Sounds of hammering came to him from way down the hill, and then a *boom*. A crew was clearing debris at the mine, making ready for work to go on.

He must have fallen asleep. He woke to a dream.

An old woman knelt beside him, a blanket pulled up over her head like a cloak. She spoke. "Clem."

Startled, he sat up straight. His breath hissed.

"Clem."

She pulled back the blanket, and he saw her face, scabbed and dirty.

He *must* be asleep. A dream! But—

"Are you a ghost?" he asked.

She shook her head.

"You're not a ghost?"

She punched his shoulder. "No, dummy, I'm not a ghost. It's me!" When he made no move and sat still as stone, she leaned to him and grabbed his arms and shook him. "It's me."

Lindy! It was *Lindy*!

He threw his arms around her, toppling her. "Everyone thinks you're dead!" he cried. "We looked everywhere! My guts were in my throat every time I dug through a new pile of rubble, thinking I'd find your dead body!" He pulled away and looked at her. "You're not dead!"

They laughed, she sat up. Her breath was bad. He wondered how she'd been taking care of herself. She told him how she was thrown by the wind, but landed gently.

"For a tornado, I mean." She glanced away. "You mad at me?"

"No! No, I'm not mad! I might be mad, but I'm—I'm just so glad I hardly know what to say!" He leaned to her, their foreheads touched. He put his arms around her and pulled her close. "It was horrible, you being dead."

He put his hands on her cheeks and tipped her face to him. He wanted to kiss her, to trace her scar with his fingers, but he felt suddenly shy. There was plenty of time. That's what he'd told her when he went to find her that night. His heart was pounding, and there was plenty of time.

"Otto's dead," he told her. "And Pally-boy." She squeezed his hand, and he couldn't stop looking at her, her hands, her hair, her face.

"You know, your scar looks kind of like a map of Missouri," he said.

Her shoulders dropped, and she stared at him. "Did you just say my scar looks like a state map?"

He nodded.

"You're tub-thumped."

Clem grinned, put out his hand to her. "Come on. Let's go home."

Lindy sat back. "No," she said. "No, there ain't no home for me. Clem, listen. I'm dead!" She smiled broadly, crazily. "I'm dead! I'm not here, I'm nowhere, I'm nobody!" Her eyes shone. "This is my chance! I'm free of him, and I got nobody who gives a hoot except you."

Clem stared at her.

Again she took his shoulders. "Clemmy, you're free, too. Don't you see it?

He shook his head. "I don't—"

"The mine's closed, Clem," she said. Her voice became urgent. "You see? You see what I'm saying?"

He tipped his head, squinted at her. "I'm not—"

"Clem." She scrambled to her knees, pushing the blanket out of the way, and gripped both his arms, fingers digging into muscle. "You can have your heart's desire. Look at me. You can get out of the mine. This is how you get out."

He took a sharp breath.

"The trains are coming and going like gangbusters," Lindy went on. "A relief train's leaving this afternoon, bound for St. Louis. We can get on it, easy. I got my secret money, and we can go."

His ears rang. Colorful pictures whirled around in his head. No more going down the deep dark. No more stink of carbide.

"Run! Run with me! Can't you see us, Clem?"

He rose to his feet and felt the spinning of his world.

"Yes! Yes, we'll go together!" He could swear he saw a couple of birds fly up and away on the wind, singing! Cardinals? Singing!

"I'll go and find my mama," Lindy said. "I'll find my little brother or sister." She was beaming, so confident she seemed transformed. Her "death" had changed her into someone with hope. Real hope. Clem's head was spinning with possibility. He put his hands out, and she took them.

"We'll be our own family," she said. "A real family."

Something shifted inside, at the word. Family. Something settled, sank.

Lindy gripped his two hands. "Train leaves at 3:10."

His family. Grampy's terrible coughing, even worse since the tornado, and Ma's broken tooth. Pap was on the mend, and even helping Ma around the house, but still he was weak. The flimsy rolled-tin roof, the ore underground, the cage, the work, the graves—all the reasons why he could not go.

The sun shifted to one side of the sky, darkening the day. Shadows stretched and the arriving train whistled, long and low. A crew clearing rubble at the mine issued a final-sounding *boom*. The tornado of wild excitement and gladness that had tossed him around inside dropped him where he stood and suddenly, simply, died out. He stood there numbly holding on to Lindy's hands. Gently, he let go.

"Clem?"

He pulled her to him, and held her. Over her shoulder, he saw the wrecked school. This was where he was supposed to quit being a boy, that last day of class. But he hadn't, not that day. This, then, was the day he was to quit being a boy. It hurt. It hurt to turn his back on this chance.

21

GLÜCKAUF

IT WAS LIKE losing her all over again. He'd tried to talk her out of going to St. Louis alone, tried to convince her to come live with them, or maybe Miss Pipe—but she insisted she would go. And she was right to; her daddy would never let her be. Clem swore he'd never tell, and she'd gone to wait, alone and in secret, for the train.

Now Clem stood on a stool, a piece of paper in his hands, and looked out over the people gathered in the Pullman railroad car, a crude church; sober-faced miners come to pay respects to one of their own: Ma, working her jaw, probing with her tongue her broken tooth; Pap, leaning heavily on a cane; Otto's mother in a yellow dress, like she wore that day. He could picture her, arms outstretched, joyfully calling her son's name, thinking the danger was past. Miss Pipe stood very straight beside her farmer, clutched a Bible, and quietly wept.

Clem read from his paper now, words he'd written about Otto, what a steady miner he was, what a hard worker. He talked about Otto's days at school as a ballplayer, left field, how when he chose up teams he always picked the worst guy first. People smiled, nodded, yes, a good boy, a good man.

"Miss Pipe assigns a theme paper at the end of every year," Clem said, "two hundred fifty words beginning *I believe.*"

He thought of Lindy, pressed his lips together to gather his feelings. She had decided to believe she could go and find a better life.

Purdy-purdy-purdy! A cardinal sang through the open windows of the Pullman. *Make a wish, Clemmy!* He could almost hear Esther's voice.

All the air seemed to go out of him, and he felt weak and hopeless. Absently, Clem folded his paper, corner to corner.

Purdy-purdy-purdy! The song moved farther away.

Esther was dead, and Otto, and Pally-boy, and the rest. Clem was alive, he thought, alive to do his work and to take care of Ma and Pap and Grampy. That's why he couldn't go. He figured his decision was one a man would make.

He slipped the paper into his pants pocket, and took a breath.

"You want to know what Otto wrote on his theme paper? What he believed?" he said. "Otto believed in the miner's code. Work hard, hope for a bit of luck, and get out alive. Otto died—but he got out alive every day." It hadn't come out right, and Clem shifted his feet and glanced apologetically at Mrs. Pickens. "What I mean to say is, he lived the way he meant to live, every day, every time around. Decently."

Clem stepped to one side, felt grit slide beneath his

boots. "You know, I was kind of mad at Miss Pipe for writing only *Good Luck* on my final essay. It seemed a hollow thing for her to say, when she knew where I was headed. I balled up that theme paper and pitched it in the prickers." He shook his head, looked at the closed casket. Lindy's grave hadn't any casket buried in it, but she had a limestone marker, just like all the others who were gone. He pictured her sitting on that train, heading to a new life.

"Otto said 'Good luck' the miners' way—'*Glückauf*'—at the start of every shift, like a prayer, with all his heart. *Glückauf*. I think the very best we can do is wish each other good luck, and . . . and hold on tight."

The Pullman car was quiet.

Purdy-purdy-purdy. It didn't matter which way the cardinal flew, Clem wanted to tell Ettie. It's up to us to decide.

"If I wrote my theme paper again, now," Clem said, "I'd keep it pretty simple." He looked at his family, and Miss Pipe, and sent a thought to Lindy, by now somewhere west of Bonne Terre. "I believe you have to shine your own light, and not just in the mine. Somewhere in there with luck and hope and wishing, there's just you, whoever you are, shining your own light, wherever you happen to be.

"So—I'll say it now, to all of you, for Otto Pickens. *Glückauf*. Good luck, and to grass.

"I liked your talk."

Clem turned and saw a man, a stranger. There had been lots of strangers in Leadanna since the tornado. He was tall, but stooped under the weight of a large leather satchel, the broad strap of which crossed his chest. He had a wide stance, feet splayed outward, his upper body leaning forward as if in eagerness. He wore a city hat.

"In there," the man said. "Your talk, your speech, about your friend."

"Oh. Thanks." Clem started to walk on in the direction of the mine. He would go and help clear the way for work to begin.

"I'm from the paper. The *Post-Dispatch*."

Clem stopped. People streamed out of the Pullman car, coming and patting Clem's shoulder, shaking his hand, murmuring comfort, winding and circling around him, as if he and the stranger were fixed in the center of a wheel.

"That was lovely," Miss Pipe said, her gaze moving between Clem and the stranger.

"He's from the paper," Clem said, to explain.

"Ma'am." The man tipped his hat.

"It was a lovely eulogy, wasn't it," she said. "Clemson was the best student I ever had in my class." Clem studied his feet. Then Miss Pipe put her arms around him and hugged him. "I miss you at school," she said into the side of his neck. Then she pulled away, held him at arm's length for a moment, nodded to Clem and to the newspaper man, and walked away.

"I got stories'll liketa curl your hair!" Old Saw said.

"Fine, that's fine," the man said, agreeable.

"Just ask young Clemson, here, he'll tell ya!"

"I believe it."

Mrs. Pickens came and took Clem's hands in hers, thanked him.

Then the way was clear, and Clem nodded to the man and made to leave.

"Maybe you can help me," the man said.

Clem paused. "Sure," he said. He watched Old Saw gesturing wildly at Miss Pipe, probably telling her some grim story.

"And maybe I can help you," the man said.

Clem turned toward him, and the man took a few wide, lunging steps with his duck-like walk.

"I'm down here for the *St. Louis Post-Dispatch*, like I said, taking photographs, before-and-afters. The paper set up a disaster fund."

Clem stared at him. "We appreciate it."

"Well," the man wagged his head, "I'm being honest with you, now, subscriptions are up. Significantly up. What's bad for you down here, to us is mother's milk."

Clem looked past the man's shoulder, at the heaps of debris.

"We're looking for the personal stories. Like your eulogy in there. It's painful, it's heartfelt, anyone can see that. *To grass,* all that. Our readers want to know all about it. Everything you've got to say."

Clem brought his focus back to the man's face, his words. *Everything you've got to say.* Clem repeated it in his mind.

"All your stories."

He stood there, dumbly. Pictures jumped inside his head. Pally-boy biting Moonshine's leg in the night; Lindy's rubbery scar, slick with tears; Esther's pale hair spread across a white pillowcase; Pap half-crushed under the slab; Miss Pipe's books.

The man fished in his front coat pocket, pulled out a business card, held it out. Clem took it.

"When the cat gives your tongue back, you let me know, all right?"

Clem stared from the card to the man, back to the card, where a name was printed: Mr. Abel Jamison. Still Clem didn't speak.

Away up the hill, the lone bull pine shivered gently, the very top of it catching a high breeze. The chat mountain still stood solid as stone; but, up there, so did that lone bull pine. Clem guessed even something as terrible as a tornado could bring with it something different. With the bad, maybe, some good.

"I—I was down the mine," Clem said in a rush. "When it happened." He swallowed hard.

The photographer tipped his hat back with his finger. Then he removed his hat altogether and set his satchel down. "You're a miner, then?"

The question hung there, high and heavy, like Pap's sledge above the fluorite crystal.

"Yes," Clem said. Then, "No." He shifted his weight side to side. His boots felt too tight.

Mr. Jamison rubbed the back of his neck. "So you're not a miner?"

Clem glanced over at Pap, leaning on his cane and talking with Mrs. Pickens. "I'm—I'm a kid."

The man settled his hat back on his head. "Mm-hmm. All right. Well, kid"—he tapped the card in Clem's hand—"don't lose that. I want to hear from you." He hefted his bag onto his shoulder again and bounced lightly up and down, adjusting the weight of it. "Duty calls. I'm on deadline."

Clem watched the man walk away.

"Hey!" Clem hollered. His heart skipped a beat. "Hey!"

Mr. Jamison turned back, waited.

"Does it—does it pay?"

Mr. Jamison grinned. "Mr. Pulitzer pays best in the industry—fair pay per story, fifteen dollars a week on staff," he called. "If you're any good." He tapped the brim of his hat, turned, and walked on.

Miss Pipe said I was good, Clem thought. His heart beat fast. Clem stuffed his fists into his pockets and walked around the chat dump to the mine.

By the time the month of May ran down, work was in full swing at the American B, and most of Leadanna had been rebuilt. Miller's was bigger than before, and the Tunnel Tavern was bright and clean, and Lonnie was back pouring coffee at Travers' All-Day Breakfast most mornings. One sunny afternoon on his day off, Clem was perched up high on a roofline of the new church, nails pinched between his lips, hammering a shingle, when he heard the sound. Sun beat down on him like a bellows and he sat back on his heels and wiped his forehead with the back of his wrist. Light blinded him. He blinked.

He heard the sound again—a long, low note. He squinted at something coming south along the railroad tracks. The sun made heat waves in the air; it was difficult to see. But what he saw made his chest ache: an animal, lurching down the tracks on short, stubby legs, one of them pulled up close to its hind end, long matted hair, sharp muzzle.

No. Clem took a breath. No. He didn't dare let himself think it. He shut his eyes against the stinging behind his lids, and he pressed his lips together. He took a breath and held it.

"Young Clemson?"

Clem opened his eyes and stared into Old Saw's waxen face, his sunken cheeks and rotted teeth. Concern drew a line across the old man's brow. "You hain't going to faint, now, are you?"

Clem wanted to see around Old Saw, to the broken landscape below the building going up, to look again. "I might," he said. Clem waited for the grim fainting story that was sure to come out of Old Saw's gash of a mouth.

"Ha-well," the old miner said. He stared at Clem a long moment. Took off his hat and combed his hair with his fingers, fanned Clem with the hat for a second, then put the hat back on. "I'll grab you, if you do."

"Okay," Clem said, surprised. Old Saw shifted his scarecrow frame, and Clem looked down below. Nothing. He squeezed his eyes closed again. He breathed.

He slid down the roof, stepped down the ladder, and dropped, feet hitting heavy on the ground. Then, behind him, he heard a whisper of a bark, and his nose felt the pressure of tears. Clem gripped the sides of the metal ladder, something hard and real, then slowly turned.

The dog was injured. He stood there balanced on three legs. But it was him. Clem was almost sure of it.

"Pally-boy?" Clem dropped to his knees and opened his arms. The dog whisper-barked again and ran his muzzle all over Clem in a fit of joy. It *was* Pally! He made it back! He came back!

Clem threw himself on Pally-boy and held on tight. He pulled away again and looked Pally all over. Pally grinned, like he had that first day he came up on the porch and took them all in. Clem wrapped his arms around him again and kissed his mangy head.

"That your dog?"

Clem looked up at Old Saw, above him on the roof. "It sure is," Clem shouted. "The tornado took him, but he found his way back. Look at him! Just look at him!"

Old Saw removed his hat and scratched the top of his head. "That th'here is quite a story," he said at last. "That's a good one."

A shiver ran across the back of Clem's shoulders, and he thought of Abel Jamison handing him his card. It was like hope, Pally was, limping back into his life.

"I have to go!" he called to Old Saw. He couldn't wait to show Grampy and Ma and Pap that Pally-boy'd come home.

22

THE EVENING NEWS

"PAP! MA! LOOK at this! Grampy, come and look at this!"
Clem burst into the house waving the evening newspaper.

It was a small story in the *St. Louis Post-Dispatch,* one
and a half columns on page six, titled "The Return of
Pally-boy." Ma hugged him and kissed him, and Grampy
patted him on the shoulder.

"And look at this!" Clem flapped an oblong paper high,
and then handed it over to Pap with a happy flourish.

Pap scowled. "What's this?" He was sitting at the table,
and spread around him were his rifle, the disassembled parts
of his cap lamp, carbide tins, his boots.

"It's a check. A paycheck."

"They paid you for it?"

"Yessir!"

"Well," Pap said. Clem could fairly see Pap's thoughts.
"It's not a thing you can count on, see," Pap said. "You
can count on the Ozarks Lead Belt running under our very
feet, Clemson. That's work you can count on and be proud
of." He rubbed a dingy cloth across the Justrite reflector,

around and around, and looked accusingly at Clem. Clem swallowed what felt like a lump of chert in his throat.

Pap loosely assembled the lamp and set it on the table. In the reflector, Clem could see the hard line of Pap's jaw, whisker-shadowed. Pap was getting ready to go back to work, starting slow. He'd never recovered full use of his legs, and no one was sure he'd ever work a full shift again in his life.

"It's fine work you done, Clemson J," Ma said. "You want something to eat? I feel like a celebration is in order, don't you, Clem?" She squeezed Pap's shoulder. Pap only grunted, reaching for the big Shawinigan tin, and began to fill his carbide flask. Two shots. "How about I make up a chocolate cake."

Clem felt his stomach clench. The newspaper lay on the table by Pap's heavy boots. Pap wasn't even going to read it. Clem's old anguish rose up in him again. Pally-boy seemed to sense the change in Clem, and came and pressed against his leg.

"Pap, why'd you smash that crystal I found?"

Silence. "What?"

"Why'd you do it?"

Slowly Pap screwed the cap onto his milk-bottle flask, his eyes not moving from Clem's face. Grampy and Ma were silent and still.

All at once, Pap stood and pushed aside the equipment that littered the table. His flask fell to the floor and banged. "You think you're too good for it, is that it? You think you're better than me?" He threw the check aside and lowered his head like a bull. "You're just like Jasper."

Ma took a breath, and her hand went to her chest.

"I am!" Clem shouted. "I am like him! All I know of my real daddy is he didn't want to end up a miner, and neither do I. That's all I know of him!"

Grampy shifted in his chair. "He was the better looking of the two, remember," he said loudly.

Pap shot him a dirty look, in no mood for jokes, then swung his head back to Clem. "Jasper was biggity. He had the pretty girl, and he was too good for the mines, just like you."

Ma, a pretty girl? Clem looked at her. Her eyes behind her glasses looked frightened and she clutched at her apron. He took a deep breath.

"It's not I'm too good for it, Pap. It's honest work, I know that. Some people like it, even. Otto liked it! But not me. I want to do something different. I can't stay down the deep dark my whole life, I just can't! I wish you would take a look at me and see I'm different than you, that's all."

"My son would be a miner!" Pap roared. "That's all I got to say about it!" He brought his fist down on the table. His lamp bounced once and fell to the floor. Pally-boy jumped and danced, whining pitifully. The light, quick sound of the lamp breaking apart chimed in Clem's ear.

Ma got down on the floor and began to pick up the lamp parts. Clem thought of her picking through Esther's treasures on the floor of his room, and dropped to his knees to help her. He felt sick.

Then Ma stood and took off her apron and hung it on the peg, her movements slow and deliberate, and quietly she walked out of the room. Pap reached up and put the rifle in the hooks above the door, cursing under his breath.

When Ma came back into the kitchen, she carried with

her a sheaf of papers. She cleared her throat and set out the papers on the table at Pap's place.

"Sit down, Clem," she said.

Pap stared at her, seemed to make some objection on principle, but she pinned him with her gaze and he lowered himself into his chair.

She turned to Clem and adjusted her eyeglasses on her nose. "They were in Ettie's treasure box." She clasped her hands over her heart, then opened them to him, as if releasing birds. "You were a good brother to her."

"Clemson's got things to say, and he's got a way to say 'em," she said, turning to Pap. She brushed her fingertips across the pages of Clem's stories, inked in midnight blue. "They make me feel closer to our daughter, because she treasured 'em, and closer to our son, because he wrote 'em." She squared the pages on the table in front of Pap, neatening the corners, then gestured to the stack.

Pap didn't move to take the stories, and his jaw was set hard as the east-west road.

Ma tried again. "I've asked a lot of you, Clem, I know I have." Pap shook his head. She held up a hand to quiet him, placed it on his shoulder. Clem wondered if she meant because he'd married her, because he'd been a father to her baby. "I ask this, too."

Pap looked at her a long moment; then he nodded and dropped his dark chin, picked up the first sheet of paper. He studied the words, squinting as if they were written in a foreign language.

Quietly, Ma picked up Pap's boots from the table and set them on the floor beside the door. Clem cleared away the Shawinigan and the lamp parts, and Pap read silently.

"This won't do," Grampy yelled. Pap's head jerked. "I want to hear 'em read out loud. And I mean loud! I don't hear so good!"

Pap looked at Clem and then set the paper on the table. He pushed his chair back, crossed his arms over his broad chest, and closed his eyes. Ma coughed lightly.

"Clemson J, why don't you read your stories to us," Ma said. "Go ahead, now."

Clem sat at the table. He picked up the first story, the one about the cardinal singing to the princess, and fought back a fluttery feeling in his chest. Coals sighed and shifted in the cookstove.

Ma leaned over Pap and brushed the hair from his forehead. "Clem, are you going to sleep, or are you going to listen?"

Pap didn't move an inch. "I'm listening," he said. He opened one eye and looked at Clem, closed it again. It wasn't a wink. Definitely not a wink. But. It was a change, Clem thought. He felt it, something softening, breaking apart, shifting and settling, like those coals in the stove. He took the story in his hands and began to read, his voice plenty loud.

That night, waiting happily for sleep to come, Clem went over every detail of the wonderful night. Sitting around the table, Clem had read aloud every story Esther had kept. Pap didn't interrupt, he didn't roll his eyes, he didn't snort or sigh. He simply sat, still and quiet, and listened.

"Clem's stories are mighty pleasing, wouldn't you say?" Ma touched Pap's shoulder.

Pap stirred. "How would I know? I was never much for reading and pondering," he said. "Clem would be the one to know if it's good." He shrugged. "I'm no judge."

Clem wanted to laugh. Pap? No judge? He peered at him. Was he kidding? Clem had always thought Pap the judge of everything he did, every step he took, every word he said that came out wrong. Now, in the low light of the kitchen at evening-time, he looked again. Here was Pap listening quietly to the stories Clem had written, and saying he was no judge. Here he was saying that Clem would know best.

In the morning when Clem got out of bed and pulled the curtain, his chest filled and fluttered with pride, happiness, and hope. He looked out the window at the thin light and believed what was dawning was truly a brand new day, one that shone on Pap and Clem a different light that would only grow brighter. He got up and got some clean paper, and the pen Ettie'd given him on his birthday; his hand hovered over the page. There was the story about the ghost dog, and one about the fool's gold, and another about the cave pearl. And there was the story about Grampy's miners' consumption, and the weekly letters to the St. James Lead Company. Clem wrote that story first, and very carefully.

In the weeks that came along and carried them deep into another summer, Clem worked the mine, Pap took a few short shifts, and the *St. Louis Post-Dispatch* ran three more stories. Each time, Clem gave the paycheck to Pap with a mixture of pride and restless longing.

And then, late one bright afternoon, Clem heard loud

bellows ranging up and down, up and down; after tolerating several loud, sour notes, he realized that the noise was coming from Grampy. He pulled back the kitchen curtain and saw the old man out by the road. He was waving a paper up over his head, high-stepping all around the mailbox, and singing in a voice as tuneless and off-key as Lindy's whistling.

"I got my compensation! I got my compensation!"

Pally-boy was right beside him, hopping and yipping and biting the air as if he might catch sunlight in his teeth.

A second piece of mail, just as sweet, arrived in the box that day—a letter from Lindy up in St. Louis. She had got a job in a shirt factory, and she'd seen his stories in the newspaper. *I am glad to learn how Pally-boy found his way home to you. That is some good dog. I have not found my mama yet, nor any little sister or brother. The work is hard, but it's my own.* The letter was signed *Your Friend Lindy.* A postscript read: *I miss you something fierce.*

Clem folded the letter and put it in his pocket, beside the handkerchief he always carried.

23

TO GRASS

HIGH CLOUDS SKITTERED across the chunk of sky over Leadanna between the chat dump and Goggin Mountain, blocking the sun one moment, revealing it the next, so that light fell in thick columns reeling with dust from the mill.

Clem stood on the platform beside Ma and Pap and Grampy and Pally-boy.

"It's late, I think," Clem said.

"How's that?" Grampy cocked his head, hand to ear.

"I said the train's a little late."

Clem looked up and down the platform, ran a finger in between his new, white shirt collar and his scrubbed neck.

"There!" Grampy pointed.

The train appeared in the distance.

The train came closer, sounding louder, huffing and chugging, slowing, *screeeeeee*. The whistle blasted, moaned as it dropped away. Rail cars—big and black and hissing— pulled up and slowed, and finally parked their massive bulk beside the small station. *Hssssssssss. Ch-ch-chiiih hisssss.*

Ma was saying something Clem couldn't hear.

He leaned closer. "What?"

"I tell you, Clemson Jasper Harding, we'll just miss you something awful."

Clem's stomach lurched and went hollow, as if the platform had suddenly dropped out from under his feet, like the cage falling into the mine shaft. With the St. James Lead Company checks to provide for them, and Pap working short shifts, and with Ma's encouragement, a door in Clem's mind blew wide open and threw light all around. Clem thought how he made his way in the dark of the mine, shining his light as far as it would go, sometimes just barely enough to keep moving forward. Right now he could see only as far ahead as the office of the *Post-Dispatch* and the city of St. Louis. It was enough to go by.

Hssssssssshhhh.

Leaving wasn't how he'd imagined, all along, when he'd pictured what it would be like to stand up to Pap and quit the mines and get out. It wasn't ever like this mix of excitement and fear, elation and sorrow. He'd stood up to Pap, in a way, but it had been a gentle way—only by reading out his stories in a voice no louder or stronger than his own. Clem's standing up was as much Pap standing down, with Ma and Grampy there to guide them both.

Bo-ard! Board!

"Oh, Clemmy," Ma said.

He held tight to her hand. She kissed him, stroked his cheek.

"I'll find you a cave pearl, Ma," he said.

She smiled. "I know you will."

Bo-ard! All aboard!

Pap shook Clem's hand and left forty-five dollars in his grip. "You earned it," he said. He placed a firm hand on Clem's shoulder and looked him in the eyes a long moment. "You do have Jasper's eyes," he muttered. Then he winked. "But you've got my stubborn streak." Then all in a rush he dropped his cane and pulled Clem to him roughly and spoke in his ear, his voice trembling with emotion. "You earned it, son."

Clem knelt and Pally step-hopped to him and buried his gray muzzle in Clem's neck. Clem hugged Pally-boy, breathing in the tang of his thick fur till he thought he might break. Then he stood and willed himself not to cry.

"Don't worry about us," Grampy said. He nodded firmly, his eyes wet and shining. "Go on and get. You don't want that train leaving without you." He grabbed Clem in a hug.

Clem boarded the train and found a seat by a window. In the end, everything seemed to happen slowly, but quickly, too; the train whistled, and then it simply pulled away, with him on it. He leaned out the window and waved. They all waved, Ma, Pap, Grampy, Pally-boy's tail, until the train rounded the chat mountain and passed through the shadow it cast, and the town fell away from sight.

Clem sat back against the hard bench seat, reached inside his pocket and withdrew Lindy's handkerchief. He smoothed the embroidered square on his lap, folded it, pressed it to his cheek. He put it in the chest pocket of his smart new coat, beside Mr. Jamison's card with the address of the *St. Louis Post-Dispatch*, and when he did, he noticed a few small white spots on his fingernail beds. He remembered another day, a long time ago, when Esther took his hands and told his fortune. A gift, a ghost, a friend, a foe, a letter to come. A journey to go.

The train took Clem quickly out of the swath scraped and torn by the tornado, into landscape he'd up to now only glimpsed in the distance from the top of Goggin Mountain, speeding on through woods of black oak and silver maples, through mountain laurel pink and fragrant, faster and faster, pounding alongside pure white limestone ledges under which, he knew, silent gray bands of ore waited for someone to find. But not Clem. He looked out the wide window of the train and felt the beat of wheel on rail, going on, going away, going north. Going to grass.

AUTHOR'S NOTE:

Whistle in the Dark is a work of fiction, though based in part on actual places and events.

Leadanna was a real place on the map, a settlement along a spur of the Missouri Pacific Railroad. If you were to travel there now, you would see the abandoned track bed; cracked concrete foundations at the site of the mine; the rise of the old chat dump, capped years ago; and a single smokestack, once 125 feet high, now lying on its side in three pieces, oak trees growing up between. You'd find no people there.

The real Leadanna was a shanty town, thirty-odd shacks and a company store. For modern comforts—street system, water system, school—you'd have had to travel a half mile to neighboring Annapolis, which boasted a brick two-story schoolhouse, a hotel, and two mansions. And while other lead mines along the Southeast Missouri Lead Belt were up to date, with electric lights and elevators, the mine at Leadanna was primitive: no power but the mules and the men.

If the real Leadanna was so different from Clem's Ozark hamlet, why not give the fictional town some other name? Simply, I liked it. I like how the mining product, the object of Clem's torment, stands grimly at the front: *Lead*. And then, a twist around the middle brings about the murmuring *anna*, like longing, like *away*, which is, in part, Clem's heart's desire. Leadanna seemed the right place for Clem's story to happen, and I hope I'll be forgiven my many liberties.

Hazards of mining were very real. Contemporary newspapers such as the *Lead Belt News* commonly ran gritty accounts of accidents and fatalities like the ones Old Saw tells Clem. Miners' consumption, or "miners' con," from which Grampy suffered, was a condition in which silica dust from mining invaded the miners' lungs, making it more and more difficult to breathe.

The tornado, too, really happened. On March 18, 1925, the Great Tri-State Tornado touched down near Leadanna, wiping out about two-thirds of the houses plus all the mine structures and hoisting machinery. The tornado followed the path of the Southeast Missouri Lead Belt, along which several small mining towns were completely destroyed, then jumped the Mississippi River and ripped through Illinois and Indiana until, more than three hours and 219 miles after it began, the mile-wide cyclone finally petered out. Nearly 700 people were killed; it is considered the deadliest tornado in U.S. history.

Readers interested in Ma's superstitions might enjoy Vance Randall's books, among them *Ozark Magic and Folklore*.

Readers who want to get a sense of the tornado from firsthand accounts are directed to Wallace Akin's *The Forgotten Storm: The Great Tri-State Tornado of 1925* and Peter S. Felknor's *The Tri-State Tornado: The Story of America's Greatest Tornado Disaster*.

ACKNOWLEDGMENTS

Many people helped me write this book by offering cheer and inspiration, insightful readings, tricks, treats, sticks, carrots.... I thank especially Sarah Brune, Heather Vogel Frederick, Heather Henson, and Natalie Serber. Dustin Walker and Lester Ruble provided helpful information about the settlement of Leadanna and the Great Tri-State Tornado, and Mike Ausec shared his knowledge of old-time mining and mining equipment, and the anecdote on which the crystal incident is based. Any errors are my own.

Encouragement came at a critical time when early chapters received a Katherine Paterson Prize; subsequent publication in the journal *Hunger Mountain* brought the attention of agent Heather Schroder, and then editor Sylvie Frank, who both worked patiently and enthusiastically for as long as it took. Thank you, Heather; thank you, Sylvie! And I hope that if Katherine Paterson reads the rest of the story, she'll think it holds up.

I couldn't have written a word if not for my family: my husband, Matt, *sine qua non* and our daughters Molly and Eliza, *semper ubi sub ubi*.